LEAVING LETITIA STREET

Jacqueline Simon

LEAVING

LETITIA

STREET

STORIES

Braeswood

Houston

Published by Braeswood Books, Houston 77025

Printed in the United States of America

Library of Congress Control Number: 2019938982

Publisher's Cataloging-In-Publication Data

Names: Simon, Jacqueline, 1943- author.
Title: Leaving Letitia Street : stories / Jacqueline Simon.
Description: First edition. | Houston : Braeswood Books, [2020] | Several stories
previously published in Redbook, Ploughshares, Domestic Crude, the Literary
Magazine of Houston, and Her Work: Stories by Texas Women.
Identifiers: ISBN 9781732352902 (hardcover) | ISBN 9781732352919 (softcover) |
ISBN 9781732352926 (ebook)
Subjects: LCSH: Families--Fiction. | Man-woman relationships--Fiction. | Love--
Fiction. | LCGFT: Short stories. | Domestic fiction.
Classification: LCC PS3619.I5621 L43 2020 (print) | LCC
PS3619.I5621 (ebook) | DDC 813/.6--dc23

Leaving Letitia Street is a work of fiction. Any references to actual
events, real people, or real places are used fictitiously.

Designed by 1106 Design
Cover painting (detail) by Walter Taylor, 1860–1943. Private collection.

"Envoy" from BALLISTICS: POEMS by Billy Collins, copyright 2008
by Billy Collins. Used by permission of Random House, an imprint and
division of Penguin Random House LLC. All rights reserved.

First Edition

For Jim Colthart

Go, little book,
out of this house and into the world,
. . . .
stay out as late as you like,
don't bother to call or write,
and talk to as many strangers as you can.

—BILLY COLLINS

CONTENTS

LEAVING LETITIA STREET

SISTERS

*W*hen I was a child I took piano lessons from my Aunt Gabrielle. She taught me the scales, the progressions of chords, the position of the hands. "The fingers must rest lightly over the keyboard," she said. "Thumbs are not straight"—she bent my thumbs into their proper crook—"and wrists are up. Staccato comes from the arms, not the wrists. From the arms!" She demonstrated with a Beethovian attack on the keyboard. "You must feel it here," she said, pressing both of her hands against her chest. "It keeps the bosom firm." Her bosom was very large and firm. "Will it make my bosom big?" I asked. "Yes," she promised, "if you practice at least three hours a day." It did not affect my bosom—I was ten years old at the time—but then I didn't practice three hours a day, either.

Sometimes I stayed at her house when my parents went out of town. Gabrielle not only played the piano, she sang opera. She sang with all the windows of the house open, because she liked fresh air. The neighbors heard arias from *Così fan tutte* and *La bohème.* Gabe was a coloratura; she could sing a high E as pure as holy water. *Mi piaccion quelle cose che han si dolce malia.* "I love all things that have a gentle magic." As she sang Mimi's song, she flung open windows, she heaved her ample bosom. *Che parlano di sogni e di chimere, quelle cose che han nome poesia*: "That speak of dreams and fancies, the things called poetry."

And the neighbors next door would turn up their radio. Letitia Street had changed over the years, and the neighbors weren't what they used to be. "Such a shame," Gabe said when I mentioned the radio. "They don't know music. Listen!" We listened, for a moment, to the top tune of the day—Patti Page asking, "How much is that doggie in the window?"—and then Gabe would really let go: *"Il primo sole è mio, Il primo bacio dell'aprile è mio!"* That was 1953, before anybody had stereo, and my Aunt Gabrielle could drown out the likes of Patti Page without half trying.

In her youth, Gabe had wanted to be a great performer, either as a singer with the Met or as a concert pianist. "I could have made it as either," she confided, "though you wouldn't know it now, to listen to me. But when I was in practice . . ." It's easy to deceive oneself about such things, but Gabrielle's dreams seemed possible. She had been the leading soprano with the New Orleans Grand Opera Company; her voice had been heard throughout the South. "Professor Pilar knew I had it. He said I could have made it in New York."

Professor Pilar had been her teacher, a Dutch Jew in his seventies whose body, as frangible as a sparrow's, housed a giant in the defense of talent. He had come from The Hague to escape the war; before that, he and his wife had been at the Paris Conservatory. His brother, another émigré, played with the Boston Pops.

"Professor Pilar knew his music," Gabe said. "He used to tell me, 'Gabrielle, you are one in a thousand. One in ten thousand.'"

"So why didn't you go to New York?"

"My sister. She didn't want me to go."

"Which sister?" Gabe was my favorite aunt, but I had four other aunts on my father's side alone: two nuns, a married sister, and Aline.

"Aline. She was against it."

Aline was the oldest sister, dead now; her mass had been said when I was a very small girl.

"Why didn't you just go anyway?" I asked. I guess I should admit it; I was burning up, even then, to be a great performer myself. I would have gone to New York, I thought, sister or no sister. But of course I wouldn't have said that to my aunt.

Gabe didn't answer. I knew it made older people sad to talk about someone who was dead; my mother had taught me that. So I didn't press her, but only listened to Mimi's song: *I fior ch'io faccio, Ahime non hanno odore.* "But the flowers I make, Alas have no scent." The singing thrilled me; often I wanted to sing along, to soar with her, but I knew Gabe wanted to listen to herself, not to me. Which was all right; I was never a singer. Who could have blamed her?

As for Aline: although she died when I was very young, as I have said, there are certain things I still remember. She was immaculate, even in our small Louisiana town's sticky summers. She wore linen dresses all made from the same pattern, but each in a different color: persimmon, pink, cool blue, lilac. These dresses emitted a remote fragrance; when I stood close to her, I could detect it, the way one detects the fragrance of a plant not known for its perfume. She was like a ligustrum, which flowers even when it is clipped into a hedge.

Aline was the chief housekeeper for the rectory that adjoined Sacred Heart church. I do not mean that she cleaned house for Father Trahan—he who preached the series of sermons about St. Jerome whipping the harlot out of his room—but she supervised the maids and the cook, and she kept records of the Sunday offerings. She let me help her count the money from the offerings by putting all of the pennies, nickels, dimes, and quarters into stacks of ten. We were in a large room—it must have been the priests' library—with wide floor-to-ceiling windows which made the room cold in winter but which admitted the clear Sunday morning light. Near the door, cut flowers bloomed as though their roots were still in the earth. There were many books—*Codex Juris Cororis* would have been there, and Tanquerey's *Dogmaticae Theologiae*. Sabetti-Barret, Cardinal Mercier, Thomas Aquinas. There wasn't much furniture, except for a long mahogany table in which I could see my face reflected. Aline sat at the end of the long table, counting out dollar bills. There were many ones, few fives; it wasn't a rich parish. Still, Louisiana Catholics are devout; they gave what they had. My stacks of coins shone deep into the wood. Against one wall was a large aquarium filled with tropical fish; one of the fathers was a pisciculturist. Aline told me the fishes' names: Angels, Red Scats, one Discus with a green fluorescent stripe glowing down its side. The room was so quiet that the loudest sounds were the clinking of coins and the bubbling of the aquarium.

Aline was a fragrant memory, but Gabe was my ideal. Even before I was ten, I had decided I was going to be exactly like her. I would have a piano like hers, I would have a house like hers, I would dress like her. She had hats with pheasants' feathers, silk dresses that brushed one's arm, black patent shoes with open toes and double-octave heels. She had rings that she removed when she sat at the keyboard. My favorite was a Japanese turquoise (better, she said, than the Native American stones) that was surrounded by twenty-two garnets. The ring covered her finger down to the knuckle.

"It's vulgar," said Monet, who was Gabe's married sister. "You don't have money to throw away." Monet had a maid, a big house, and seven children. She painted roses on teacups.

"I love your ring," I whispered. It was a ring Scheherazade would wear and Lilith would covet.

"You may have it," Gabe promised, "if I ever die."

Monet didn't approve of Gabe's piano, either. One day—it was a month before Christmas, 1948, a year after Aline had died and Gabe had moved into the house on Letitia Street—Gabe decided she wasn't going to play on a spinet forever. She went down to Werlein's Music and bought a Steinway concert grand. Just like that, nine feet of piano. In 1948 a Steinway grand cost six thousand, three hundred, twenty-five dollars; Gabe didn't make that much from giving piano lessons for three years. But Aline had left her the money and Gabe was going to spend it, all of it, on a Steinway concert grand.

Monet was disgusted. "You're a fool," she said. She called in my father, who refused to participate in the argument. Monet pointed out that Gabe didn't have a room in her house big enough to hold a Steinway grand.

"I've thought of that," Gabe answered. "I'm going to knock out the dining room wall and open up the porch. Then there'll be room."

"You're wasteful," said Monet, "and you'll spend your old age in penury."

"What's penury?" I asked my father. "Is it like purgatory?"

"Very like."

"Well," Gabe said, "at least I'll have my piano in penury."

The Steinway took up all of the living room and most of the ex-dining room. The audience—when there was an audience—sat on the porch, on a tiny loveseat covered with a fringed scarf from Hawaii, a souvenir from one of Gabe's old beaus. But what a wonderful piano! Black, smooth, hard, cool, polished as an Ethiopian king. And the music! What music came out of that instrument. When my lessons were over, I would beg Gabe to play, Gershwin if we felt snappy, Chopin if we were full of sentiment. It wouldn't have mattered if the piano had stuck into the street. It was worth it. It was music.

Over the piano Gabe had hung a photograph of herself as a young girl, black-haired, black-eyed. In this photograph she stood on a stage, her arms full of roses: Maiden's Blush, Bon Silene, La Noblesse. She wore a dress of rose-colored satin, simple and severe.

But when she was giving me my lessons, in her middle age, the only performances she gave were at church.

Every Christmas Eve, at Midnight Mass, she sang "O Holy Night" with the Sacred Heart choir. When her voice floated from the loft into the nave, to mingle there with the scent and flicker of votive candles and the incense flung from the censer, when her voice rang into the silence, *O night! O night divine!*, women and men bowed their heads. Even Father Trahan, now dead several years, would have been moved to hear it.

When I was grown Gabe told me that it was Aline's earnings at our town's rectory that had supported Gabe's youthful singing in New Orleans; the New Orleans Grand Opera Company paid practically nothing. Aline's money also paid Professor Pilar. Now, Aline was the oldest in the family, nineteen years older than Gabe. Their parents had died when Gabe was only a child—their mother of a heart attack in 1922, their father a year later—and after that, it was Aline who heated Gabe's bath water and poured it into the big wooden tub in the kitchen, Aline who laid Gabe's convent dresses on her bed and saw that they were mended and clean. So, a dozen years later, when the honorariums given to Gabe by the New Orleans Grand Opera Company proved inadequate to pay for even a single room in a New Orleans boarding house, it was to Aline that Gabe naturally came for help.

"She would have given me anything she had," Gabe told me one afternoon when we were sitting over coffee. I hadn't seen her in years. She had gained weight, but her face was still smooth, unlined as an innocent's, and her hands were still those of an artist. "She would have helped me, but Father Trahan was against it."

"Father Trahan? What did he have to do with it?"

"Everything. He had absolute control over her life. I heard them talking once, when I was visiting Aline at the rectory. They were talking about me, in French."

Gabe imitated them, pursing her lips to mock Father Trahan's heavy accent. "*As ye are zealous of spiritual gifts, seek that ye may excel to the edifying of the church.*'

"'Father,'"—a soft voice here, for Aline—"'I'm sure she does nothing wrong.'

"'No doubt. But it's the temptations of that life. The temptations. Better she were here at Sacred Heart. Let her sing with our choir.'

"'She wants to go to New York . . .'

"'What if she were to go? And there meet an unbelieving man? And marry, out of the Church?'" Here Gabe lifted an eyebrow at the thought, then carried on with her impersonations.

"'She doesn't want to marry, Father.'

"'How is a young girl to know what she wants? Remember Paul. A good Catholic man is what she needs.'

"'Father—'

"'You mustn't contribute to a way of life that might jeopardize your sister's soul.'" Gabe emphasized every word of the next part. "'Do everything in your power to bring her here.'"

Then she let her face relax. "That's what they said," she finished. "And believe me, the money stopped."

"What happened then?"

"Professor Pilar was wonderful. 'You will take your lessons free,' he told me. 'Pay me what you can, when you can.' And my friends! They said, 'Get a job. Type. File.'"

She continued, "Aline bought this house I'm in on Father Trahan's advice. Oh yes, he told her how to spend her money, too! He said that she and I could live together, that I'd come home as soon as she cut off the money.

"But Professor Pilar was adamant. 'I will get you a loan,' he said. 'You'll go to New York. My brother knows people. He'll vouch for you.'

"As for Monet, she thought I should give piano lessons at the convent. 'Wouldn't that be better than typing?' she said. I tell you, everyone had his own plan for my life! But the Company said, 'Nobody sings like you, Gabe.'" She leaned back in her chair, triumphant. "I stayed in New Orleans."

"Exactly right," I said.

"New Orleans was so wonderful then! There were parties every night. We'd rehearse all afternoon and then sing in Jackson Square at four o'clock in the morning. Tourists staying out late and black people going to the markets early would stop together and watch us. They'd clap and watch us. I had a purple cotton dress with a red sash and a man from Minneapolis tried to give me his lapis ring because he said it was my color and no one else should ever wear it. That was some dress. I was in love with a boy from Loyola who lost his legs in the next war. I gave him my red sash. He had on white pants that night and a flowered Hawaiian shirt. They called them Victory shirts. Then we'd all go down to the Morning Call and have beignets and eat, eat. The sun would come up and make the Mississippi look like rosewater. It was a time."

She gathered our cups and went back for more coffee.

"Let me help," I said.

"No, everything's here." She came back and stirred my coffee the way I like it, almost white.

"The bad of it," she continued as though there were no interruption, "was that Aline blamed herself for what happened with Stanley."

"Tell me about Stanley," I said. No one discussed Stanley. In a family in which two sisters were nuns, a third sister was a respectable housewife with seven children, and the fourth had lived and worked most of her life in a rectory, there was only one appropriate intimate relationship with a man, and it lasted forever. Even the nuns, Sister Lucienne and Sister Helene, wore wedding bands; they were married to God.

"Tell me about Stanley," I begged.

"We met shortly after the war began," Gabe said, waiting for her coffee to cool. "On Sunday nights my performances were broadcast over the radio—Station WWL, fifty thousand watts, The Voice of the South."

She settled into the loveseat crowded into the corner of the room. "Now, I don't know how to explain this—a scientist might, but not me—it was over the radio that I met Stanley."

"Over the radio?"

"Yes. On a ship, in the Pacific. He was the radio officer. He picked up WWL as clear as if he had been here. I was singing *Norma*—'bel canto,' he said, '*bel canto.*' He wrote me a letter in care of the station. I still have it."

"Let me see!"

She went into her bedroom, where I heard her moving boxes in her cedar chest. When she returned, it was with a wooden box heavily carved and inlaid with yellow ivory. The letter was on top. In the faded calligraphy of a more formal generation, on thin blue paper embellished with golden anchors, the young ensign in the Pacific had written: "My dear Miss D., I have heard your singing and I admire it with all my heart . . ." He had enclosed a photograph of himself, a black and white print of an aquiline young man with eyes limpid and unsmiling, a mouth that could never lie and never kiss.

"We wrote to each other. He loved the opera, he loved my singing. He couldn't get WWL again, but he didn't forget *Norma*. As soon as he got leave—"

"He came to see you?"

"Yes. And on his next leave, we were married."

"Just like that?"

"Exactly like that. Then he went back. We wrote long, romantic letters all during the rest of the war. I prayed the rosary ten times a night that he would come home safely. And he did,"—here she smiled—"but then he wanted me to go live with him in Iowa. That's where he lived, in Iowa. On a farm!"

"You didn't want to go?"

"I had no use for a farm. What opera company is in Iowa? What radio station?"

"Surely radio stations—"

"Professor Pilar was in New Orleans. No, I didn't want to go. I thought Stanley would want to move to Louisiana. But he didn't."

"You hadn't talked about it?"

"I talked about music. He talked about my hair, my eyes. And my feet." She stretched out a foot, still the diva. "He thought I had divine toes."

Now it was my turn to smile. "So you stayed in New Orleans—"

"And he went back to Iowa. It was sad. Aline was terribly upset. Father Trahan, Sister Lucienne, Sister Helene—back home they acted as though I had died. They tried to get an annulment. There had never been a divorce in our family. Nothing worked. But I couldn't give up my singing just to go to Iowa."

"Did you still want to go to New York?"

"Absolutely. The opera broadcasts on Sunday nights were very popular. There was talk that NBC was going to contract with WWL and broadcast the performances all over the United States. Well—! This was it! You never know what could have happened. The Met? Why not? Professor Pilar was ecstatic. I was going to be another Lily Pons."

"Did NBC actually do it?"

"Yes." Gabe smoothed her hands over the old loveseat. The photograph of herself as a young girl, in the rose-colored satin dress, slender, dark-haired, beautiful, hung over the piano in counterpoint to the woman, no longer young, but still an artist, across from me now.

"NBC contracted for six performances. They were going to be broadcast live from New Orleans during the winter season. It was 1946."

"I never knew you were on NBC."

"I wasn't." Gabe looked at me. "You see, the week that the auditions started, something happened to Aline."

"What happened?"

"It was the night before my audition—the *night before.* That night Aline called long distance. I wasn't home, I was at a friend's to get a good night's sleep. My roommate stayed up all hours, reading. When I got home, she gave me the message: Aline had a lump in her breast. She was going into surgery immediately. That day."

She lifted her hands as though holding her words. "How could I sing with that? The doctors thought she might die. She wanted me with her."

"Why didn't she say anything before? Or else"—I jumped up, I practically stalked around the room—"my God, why didn't she wait one more day?"

"She didn't know."

"How could she not know?"

"I hadn't said anything." Gabe shook her head. "I wanted to surprise her."

"What about Monet? Had you said anything to Monet?"

"I don't know."

I must have looked incredulous, because she continued, "Who can remember? What difference does it make?" She pulled at the hem of her dress, too short for the current fashion. "Aline had ignored herself for years. When she finally showed the lump to Monet, you could actually see it." Gabe pushed back her shoulder and held her breast. "You could see it, a lump as big as a tennis ball."

It was scary to think of it.

"I forgot everything, I left immediately. Aline was so good," Gabe finally finished. "She never complained, not even at the end. She asked only that I be there."

The long-slanting winter light spread in the room, almost tangible. I heard Gabe's watch ticking like a metronome.

"She lived five months. I was with her every day."

For a while, neither of us talked. The light fell in shafts upon the walls, the piano, the portrait, ourselves. In the winter like that, it comes in a room so suddenly and brightly that everything seems almost to glow; then the moment is past and everything diminishes. Finally I asked, because I had to ask, "Why didn't you go back to New Orleans after she died? It was there for you. Why didn't you take it?"

My aunt looked at me, her eyes black as hours burned. "You're too young," she said.

I waited; we both knew there was a better answer.

"By the time they buried her, it was over. I had been replaced. WWL wanted me back, but NBC wasn't going to do another series." She smiled with one side of her mouth. "The first wasn't that great a success, frankly. I like to think I might have made a difference. Professor Pilar never gave up, but it wouldn't be two years before he was dead, too. No, I was here."

Gabe pushed her hands together, got up, and moved to her piano bench. She removed her rings and watch and placed them on top of the Steinway. She still had her turquoise and garnets.

"It doesn't do to talk like this," she said. I agreed. But now, in the softer light, the portrait over the piano more nearly resembled the woman at the keyboard. Her back was still straight, and her hands rested lightly on the keys, thumbs curved, wrists up.

She asked, "Would you like to hear me sing?"

IF HE COULD SPEAK
TO HIS BROTHER

*W*ard 701 is locked. If McKnight had thought about what to expect, this wouldn't have surprised him; but he hadn't thought, and it does. There's a brass doorbell, and when he rings—cautiously, like a man who's expecting a trick—it's answered promptly by a young woman in jeans. Brown, swinging hair, English complexion: McKnight takes her in at once.

"Wait right here," she tells him pleasantly, and then asks if she may take his coat. McKnight is grateful; the room feels over-heated and unhealthy. Outside, it's March, still cold, a little windy, but the sun is shining and the azaleas are out. Maybe when he leaves, McKnight thinks, he won't go back to the office; maybe he'll go for a run, finish up in the gym with a workout. Really sweat, stink a little. McKnight, recently promoted to head-office Accounting, has been working too-long hours lately. He needs the money—Lord, the bills!—but he hasn't been doing enough for his body.

Six or seven people sit or stand in the room, and trying hard to look casual, McKnight watches them. Two people are playing cards, others lounge in armchairs, one is reading and only one is obviously lost. An easy-listening Beatles' song, orchestrated for strings, whites out any street sounds that might filter up to the room, but McKnight doesn't hear the music. His hands feel as though a pint of adrenalin were pushing into each fingertip. He flexes his hands, cracking the knuckles one by one, and does discreet stomach isometrics until the young woman in blue jeans returns with Barrett.

"Who was she?" McKnight asks his brother when she has left.

"A nurse."

"Head nurse?"

"Just a nurse."

"She wasn't in uniform."

"They don't wear uniforms. To cheer us up."

McKnight nods, embarrassed. He shifts from his right foot to his left, thinking that he should have figured that out for himself.

"You want something to drink?" Barrett asks. "You want some orange juice? Soda? Carrot juice?"

"Got any beer?"

"No beer. Orange juice, soda, carrot juice, apple. Prune . . ."

"You got a grape?"

There is a grape. McKnight follows Barrett into a small, immaculate kitchen with yellow-and-lime wallpaper, a yellow counter, a pot of ivy hanging fulsomely on the wall. Plastic glasses are at the side of a stainless steel sink with a high, curved faucet. There's no stove, but the refrigerator is filled with pyramids of little cans of juices stacked by flavor.

"There must be a hundred cans in there," McKnight says, cracking his knuckles again.

"You want one or two?"

"One."

"In the can or a glass?"

"Can's fine."

"Napkin?"

"No, thanks."

"You're making all the right choices," Barrett says. McKnight is relieved; that sounds like the old Barrett.

McKnight hasn't seen his brother since Sunday morning four weeks ago, after McKnight came home from a date with the new woman in Account Forecasting. It was against his rules to play on his own turf, but Forecasting wasn't really home office, and besides, this one was all long legs and hazel eyes. She had mentioned bringing a friend, but McKnight couldn't interest Barrett. Holed up in McKnight's apartment, his wife gone off with another woman, Barrett wanted only to listen to Willie Nelson records and suffer.

Some evenings McKnight could hear his brother weeping. Barrett tried to disguise the sound by turning up the Willie Nelson records (they were left out of their jackets later and scattered all over the room), but his grief was unmistakably audible. McKnight felt he should do something helpful, but what? He advised his brother to take some extra calcium, good for the nerves; he told him to *eat,* for God's sake; to work out, to find a girl. Go back to his job. He asked Barrett, too, to please put the records back in their jackets when he was finished with them. In his bachelorhood McKnight has turned tidy.

Nothing worked. Barrett stayed in the house, a despairing, gentle, incessantly smoking ghost. "Why?" he asked McKnight again and again, leaving trails of cigarette ashes through his brother's living room, dining room, kitchen and bath. There was ash in McKnight's bed, where Barrett slept during the day, when he should have been out selling textbooks and hustling schoolteachers. "She's no more queer than you or me. Why?"

"I don't know," McKnight had said. "But it has more to do with her own problems than with anything you've done."

"You think so?"

"I know so."

Barrett was then silent for a while. He looked down at the kitchen table with the kind of thoughtfulness that made McKnight feel that at last his words might have gone home. But when Barrett finally looked up, his face was clouded.

"How can you know," he asked in a voice that was an accusation, "when she told me the opposite?"

"I know, that's all." Impatience edged McKnight's voice; he felt tense and unreasonable. "Why are you so eager to accept her blame?" he asked. "You're not to blame, Barrett! Can't you understand that?" He didn't stop when he saw his brother's jaw go rigid. "I think you want me to feel like you're some kind of wounded bird, but you're not. Quit feeling so sorry for yourself."

When Barrett stood up, McKnight thought for a moment that his younger brother was going to sock him. But Barrett said only, "You think a tablespoonful of wheat-germ oil would cure cancer. What do *you* know? You're a cold son of a bitch." He flicked a one-inch ash onto the floor and left the room.

After that, McKnight stopped giving advice. He had heard that depressed people weren't cheered by being told they were really okay. Well, Barrett was proof of that. But listening to his brother's incessant self-disparagement tried McKnight's patience—the same woe, over and over! Yet how he loved the guy! And how incredible that this love conferred no powers, made nothing easier. Perhaps, McKnight thought, he was indeed a cold son of a bitch. Beleaguered and guilty, he began spending more time away from his apartment.

When he came home Sunday morning from his date with the account forecaster, his brother was stretched out on the couch, one Willie Nelson record spinning dead-ended on the stereo, the others all over the floor. Ashes everywhere, the apartment choked with ashes. What the hell! McKnight thought, but he was in an expansive mood. Let the guy sleep; Barrett was always the big sleeper. But when his brother didn't get up for coffee and eggs, McKnight went through the motions like an unbeliever. There was a pulse, there was color, but it was a terrible color. There was an empty bottle of Seconals that only a damned fool could have missed.

Barrett opens a can of grape juice for McKnight and a carrot juice for himself. At least two dozen little cans of carrot juice remain in the refrigerator. McKnight feels better when he sees them; his brother has always been crazy for carrot juice, another self-punishment. They're taking good care of the kid, he thinks.

"This place," McKnight asks, "it's all right? You like it?" For the money, he thinks, it should be the Ritz. The bills already run to five figures, and the insurance pays only eighty per cent.

"I'll show you," Barrett says. "Let me give you the tour." He drops the two can tabs into a lime-green wicker wastebasket.

The hospital wing is decorated like a home—thick wall-to-wall carpets, table lamps, cushions and plants, original art on the walls. McKnight does not recognize the paintings as patients' art; one painting is much like another to him.

In the crafts room, Barrett picks up a piece of silver that has been hammered and tooled into the design of a flying mallard duck. "Isn't this a number to do on a perfectly good piece of silver?" he asks.

"Did you do this?" McKnight examines the metal in his hands. The work is meticulous, its own best answer to Barrett's question.

"It's a belt buckle." Barrett riffles through a stack of materials until he finds a supple piece of maroon leather. "This is going to be a belt. I haven't cut it yet."

"I *like* that," McKnight says.

"Do you? You can have it when I'm finished."

"Don't you want it?"

"Actually I was making it for you. I've made about three."

"Well, thanks." McKnight is touched and somehow embarrassed; he and his brother have not exchanged presents since they were children. "Thanks a lot," he says again.

"We have classes," Barrett explains. "In crafts." He smiles as if to show that he thinks it is all foolish. "But it passes the time."

Someone else has come into the room, someone with green eyes, blond hair, the kind of cheekbones one sees on the covers of magazines. She is wearing army fatigues—designer army fatigues—and yellow cowboy boots.

"Who's this?" she asks. She is very cheerful. "I'm Sara."

"Hi," McKnight says. "I'm McKnight. Barrett's brother."

"What kind of name is that?" Sara says accusingly. She puts her hands on her hips and smiles. "That's not your last name, if you're brothers."

"It's a first name, a family name."

"Family. Oh, that's classy," Sara says. She talks in a tough little intimate whisper. "Is yours a family name too?" she asks Barrett.

"What else? But listen," he says, "we're having a sort of private visit."

McKnight is astounded at the abruptness of this dismissal, but Sara does not seem surprised. She answers in her tough little voice: "Oh, secrets? Well." She blows them a kiss-off and leaves, taking McKnight's grape juice with her.

"Another nurse?"

"No. She's a crazy. She's driving me crazy. If that's not the pot calling the kettle." Barrett laughs. "But she's always around. You have to be here to appreciate it. I mean, I can't clean my teeth without Sara's wanting to hold the brush."

"Well, you aren't supposed to be alone," McKnight says, and immediately regrets it.

"I have to lock my door at night," Barrett says, "or she comes in. All the time. Only none of the doors here have locks, so you can't. That's why I'm not getting any sleep. They finally had to have a guard sit in a chair outside my door all night, just to keep Sara out." Barrett shakes his head. "She's a nympho. Diagnosed. At least, that's what she told me."

"No *lie*," McKnight says.

"She's a little girl. She's fourteen years old, for God's sake." Barrett brushes the hair off his forehead. "Do you want to see the game room?"

McKnight wishes Sara would come back; he's never met a certified nympho before. Such things actually happen! he thinks with amazement. A man's wife, with whom the man has never been happy, leaves and he tries to kill himself for misery; society revenges itself by locking him up with a beautiful, sex-crazed teenager. McKnight's own cross is to be average, he decides—pay the bills, vacuum the floor, watch the ball games, be grateful for account forecasters who come one's way. Yet he would wish the same for his brother, who once seemed much like him.

They walk down a wide hall where eight-foot windows, curtained in green and white checks, let in the sun. Seven stories down, Hermann Park is laid out like a landscaper's model. The trees have budded and sun penetrates their leaves, turning them transparent. McKnight can see the outdoor theater, the duck pond, the kiddie train and the zoo. He has an especially good view of the bear grotto, where the animals, larded and pacific, loll on concrete rocks or beg for forbidden treats from children who are throwing peanuts across a protective moat. From the seventh floor, the bears look like stuffed toys that the third-grade McKnight once hid from the first-grade Barrett. *You've got to get tough,* he had lectured severely. *Kids in first grade don't have baby toys. Baby, baby!* The park is swarming with kids.

Neither man has any desire to leave the window, though its checked curtains do not hide the bars.

"A guy got out last week," Barrett says, reading McKnight's mind. "He got out and jumped." He laughs, or perhaps the sound is a cough. "He fell on a ledge. Didn't kill himself, just broke himself up. They still don't know how he got out."

"They should know," McKnight says. Such inefficiency annoys him deeply, worries him. He turns to his brother. "You know you can walk out of this place any time you want to? You have that right. Whenever you want, whenever you're ready, you just call me and we'll go."

He looks at Barrett for an answer, but Barrett seems to be studying the pigeons that have taken up residence below the window. He remains at the window a long time, resting his hands on the sill. It seems to McKnight that the cooing of the pigeons is unnaturally loud.

"You just tell me," he repeats at last, feeling that he has not really said what he meant.

Barrett doesn't answer for a long time, and McKnight wonders if perhaps his brother is ready to leave right now.

He certainly sounds better, and McKnight cannot imagine why anyone would want to stay in this place. When Barrett finally says, "Poor bastard," it is a surprise.

"Who do you mean?" McKnight says. "You mean the guy who jumped?"

"Yes," Barrett says. "That's who I mean."

The tour continues, with Barrett pointing out authentic Chinese rice paper or a unique grain of hardwood paneling. He sounds like a guide promoting a historic home. Light pours through the windows. The mottled March sky and clouds resemble a Constable painting. McKnight follows from room to room, half listening. How is it, his ruminating mind asks itself, that his brother had not seen fit to tell him that he no longer had a job to return to? Barrett had turned in his letter of resignation six weeks ago, before the Willie Nelson, before the Sunday morning of McKnight's account forecaster, although Barrett's heavy books of samples, the ring-bound catalogues, remained in the back seat of his car. And after the publisher told McKnight that they would give Barrett a leave, that they would fix up his employment record for the insurance, Barrett had thanked McKnight over the phone as though he were thanking him for sending over a pack of cigarettes. McKnight could imagine his brother as he stood at the telephone, listening with no more expression than if he were listening to, say, pigeons. McKnight was hurt. He had expected—what? At least a reaction. Perhaps now, at this visit, a belated thank-you. But none is forthcoming, and McKnight follows through the rooms, his hands in his pockets, a visiting fireman from home.

They enter a room where two men are playing eight ball. The number three ball slides into the pocket when Barrett and McKnight come in, and one of the players stops to twist chalk on his cue. Taller than his companion, thin but sturdy, he wears a lumberjack shirt and brown corduroys in a style that McKnight has seen at Neiman-Marcus but passed by, hoping they will go on sale later.

"Anybody want the next game?" the taller player asks courteously. "Barrett, you want the next one?"

"This is my brother," Barrett says. "McKnight, Peter Fielding."

Fielding is as quick to shake hands as a realtor; his palm is dry and confident. He could be, McKnight thinks, any man relaxing in a country-club game room.

"Pleased to meet you," Fielding says.

The other player says nothing. His head hangs down, and he hasn't taken his eyes off the Scottish-plaid rug since McKnight came into the room. He stares at the floor, not moving, a disturbed man, visibly frightened.

But it is Fielding whom McKnight distrusts, with his well-rehearsed handshake, his smooth and manicured hands. Fielding's surface is too smooth to permit penetration. Wearing his lumberjack shirt, he could be an overworked intern; McKnight cannot tell who is patient and who is nurse, who is doctor and who is drugged. Fielding's handshake is prompt but not honest; his courtesy is a defense. It is the courtesy reserved for an outsider, for someone who will leave soon enough, to the relief of all; a courtesy for someone to whom nothing is to be revealed.

His prep-school manners, his courteous questions, even his tone of voice, remind McKnight of Barrett. His brother, whom he's taught how to ride a bike, competed against in swim meets, beaten up innumerable times, lent neckties and underwear and money, held the ring for at his wedding, whose appearance is as familiar as McKnight's own (whose significant ears, whose early-receding hairline are like McKnight's own), has disappeared under McKnight's very nose, leaving this remote stranger. His brother's courtesy is the trick for which McKnight has been waiting.

"I'm showing him around," Barrett explains to the two in the poolroom.

"Glad to meet you," Fielding repeats in his prep-school voice. "We'll save you a game later."

"Maybe later."

When they are walking back to the main room Barrett adds, as though he were pointing out an unusual view, "Pete walks around the halls at night, talking to himself. He used to be a medical student, and sometimes he thinks he's the cadaver he was assigned. He holds conversations with it."

McKnight nods, but he doesn't understand. Barrett clearly dissociates himself from these people; what is he doing among them?

In the main room he and his brother sit in two armchairs; copies of colorful magazines lie on the table between them. Nothing McKnight has said is anything he has wanted to say; his brother remains as politely distant as a tour guide. They are quiet. McKnight does not know why he can visit only once a week but he doesn't ask; his mind is loaded with questions he cannot ask. Finally he says, "You want me to bring anything special to read?"

"They don't like me to read."

"Why not? What do they expect you to do?"

"Make belt buckles. Walk around. Play pool. I talk to the shrink twice a day." Barrett gives another short laugh that is not a laugh. "Actually, I don't talk to him. He's a creep. What a creep! Comes here on his motorcycle, real loud. He parks right in front, in the circle where they're supposed to let out patients. Then he sits with me in a room for thirty minutes, waiting for me to say something. Why should I say anything? How can I talk to somebody like that? What would he understand?"

What McKnight wants to do is embrace Barrett. He wants to embrace him and take him out the door. He wants to take him home, which—McKnight has been told—is the worst place Barrett could possibly be. He remembers a question a girl once asked Barrett: Is your brother as good a man as you? No way, Barrett said, and laughed and laughed. Thanks a lot, McKnight said. You could have lied. What do you mean? Barrett said. I *did* lie.

Cheerful Sara has found them. She sits on the edge of Barrett's chair and tells McKnight, "It's nice of you to come. Nobody comes to see me."

"Her mother comes twice a week," Barrett says.

"He's so mean," Sara says, but she remains cheerful. She touches Barrett's hair and he does not move away. "Why is your brother so mean?"

At least she can do that, McKnight thinks. He cannot touch his brother's hair.

The pretty nurse who opened the door for McKnight reappears, her light-brown hair swinging easily with each step. "You'll be back next week?" she asks pleasantly, a reminder that it is time for McKnight to go.

"You'd better believe it. Listen,"—he takes Barrett's arm—"you want to walk downstairs with me? Out to the car? It's beautiful outside." He turns to the nurse. "You could come with us. Would that be all right?"

"If Barrett wants to, we could," she says. "Barrett?"

McKnight can tell she likes the idea, and he's pleased with himself for having thought of it. If he could get Barrett going, get him out . . .

"I don't know."

"We could walk over to the park."

Barrett does not answer; he looks as though the idea itself were fatiguing.

"Maybe another time," the nurse suggests gently.

McKnight cannot press further. "Let me know if you change your mind about wanting me to bring anything," he says.

"I will. And thanks for coming."

McKnight nods agreement. "It's okay. You're looking good."

"Am I?"

McKnight gives Barrett something between a shove and a hug around the shoulders. "Next week," he promises. "I'll be back."

The nurse opens the door with a key she carries on a long ribbon around her neck. In the hall McKnight is in a hospital again: green tile and the smell of antiseptic rise to meet him. The door, which had a brass, colonial-style doorknob inside, is number 701 outside, and it locks. It shuts behind him with a cushioned, metallic click. McKnight turns around. No one is looking, so he tries the handle again, just in case. The door is locked.

He is waiting for the elevator but it's slow; hospital elevators don't rush. McKnight has an urgent need to act, he needs to *move*, so he walks down the corridor very fast until he finds another door, one marked "Exit." He pushes into a concrete stairwell, and halfway down he sits on the steps. They are cold; he has forgotten his coat, but he would rather leave it than go back for it now. The stairwell has accumulated all the chill of a March morning without its sun. The cold comes through the seat of his pants until McKnight is cold clear through, but it doesn't matter; he doesn't feel it. He sits on the steps, and he weeps; he weeps until he thinks his body is coming apart.

LEAVING LETITIA STREET

On the plane coming back to Louisiana for my father's funeral, I remembered a story he used to tell when I was a child. It was this: a little girl is crossing over a bridge. There's a troll under the bridge who doesn't like little girls; any that cross over, he eats them up. But this is a brave little girl; she's determined to get over the bridge. So—at this point I am already tucked into bed, the covers tight at the sides; I scrunch under the blanket to make sure the troll can't get at me—she takes the first step over the bridge. "Who's that walking on my bridge?" the troll asks. "It's only me," says the little girl. And my father tiptoes with his fingertips across the bedcovers so I can see how scared the little girl is. "Who's that walking across my bridge?" the troll repeats. "It's only me," repeats the little girl, watching him take a few more tiptoes over the bed. And the troll begins to sway his body back and forth. My father is swaying back and

39

forth; he loves this story. And the bridge begins to sway with him. By this time my father is putting some weight into it, the whole bed is creaking, swaying back and forth, back and forth. I've got the covers up to my nose; only my eyes are out; I hardly breathe. "WHO'S THAT WALKING ON MY BRIDGE?"

"It's only me!" With this the troll can't stand any more. He jumps up, he *snaps!* his jaws together—my father is snapping his forearms, locked at the elbows—he snaps those great jaws and eats the little girl up. Agggahh! my father roars, and I am in an ecstasy of terror and pleasure. My father would make great gobbling sounds, vampire kisses, and satisfied smacking of the lips. He would pick his teeth: little girls were a great delicacy. I asked for this story every night, and every night, he told it.

I thought about that story, coming back on the plane after my father died. It was October, early in the morning. Traveling businessmen ate cold scrambled eggs and drank orange juice with vodka. The one on my right, a widower retired from real estate, kept trying to show me coin tricks. He gave me his card, The Abracadabra Man. He was a magician now, he said—did shows at grammar schools. It was a long trip; I was a thousand miles from home. Auden was right: everything turns away quite leisurely from the disaster.

The story I heard when I got home was that my parents had been playing golf, the way they had every Sunday for the last twenty years. Later that day, they were to have had friends over for bridge, two tables. But this fall Sunday, on the back nine, shortly after my father put a fifteen-yard chip shot over the sand trap and then sank a seven-foot putt for a bogie, he returned his club to the back of the cart, complained of his left arm, and said he thought he'd better go home now. It wasn't a crisis, he explained, but he was very tired and wanted to go home. A few minutes after that, he was dead.

My mother drove him back to the pro shop, holding his body against hers, jouncing the cart over roughs, cutting across fairways and even the practice greens. Somebody rounded up a doctor in the clubhouse, a young obstetrician who tried to give my mother a Valium that she wouldn't take. She stood there in the pro shop, surrounded by people and racks of knit shirts and displays of putters; and when she was finally able to say something, the doctor could hardly understand her. But I could have told him what she'd say: "Will someone please call my daughter."

My father was a man who adored women, and for a while I was the woman in his life. I lost a good deal of my advantage as I got older; you can't tickle the feet of a thirteen-year-old and throw her down, giggling, on the bed. And I grew up to be not at all what he wanted: a gawky, thin-faced kid, dark, unhappy, using time unwisely, given to evasions and deceit. I lied continually, a habit my mother

called, with varying degrees of irony, a wonderful imagina-
tion. I was a movie star, a poet, a rogue, a racehorse: I was
anything but myself. My parents couldn't figure it out. They
had put in time, love, good schools, vitamins. They went to
PTA and supervised my choice of friends. Nothing took:
and in spite of my father's stories, I wanted out. It was the
nineteen-sixties, a brand-new decade, and the world I had
grown up in was changing like a kaleidoscope. I wanted to
get a look at it.

It was my mother who gave me ideas: "Don't get married
right away," she said. "Work for a while. Learn to be on your
own. Support yourself." She herself had never taken that
advice. Married at twenty-one, she had gone straight from
her father's house to her husband's, one man to another.
My father was seventeen years older than she. He was a
gardener; she was his flower. She never had a job, never
owned a checkbook, never paid a bill or took a trip by herself.

But what she did, what he encouraged her to do, she did
well. She was a golfer: city champion. She was a fundraiser: a
new church wing went up. When she quit smoking, I thought
she was going to make the whole world quit. She bought
a film, *One in Twenty Thousand*. She bought a projector, a
screen. The movie opens with a nice guy, an ordinary guy,
strolling down the street. Camera pans to an x-ray truck.
Two minutes later, and you're watching him being cut open.
Where she got that stuff, a medical school, wherever, I never

asked. And remember, this was 1955, fourteen years before the Surgeon General's warning. The knife goes down the smooth hairless chest, I can see it, the thin line of blood following, at a second's lapse, the surgeon's hand. Cut to gloved fingers, stainless steel: they spread back the ribs, expose the grey, necrotic, breathing lung. The masks, the sounds of labored breath. I smell the anesthetic, I hear the kids in the room squirming. Because my mother took this film to my junior high school, every junior high in the city. Kids watched it, they dropped like flies, especially the jocks. Teachers hustled them out, green themselves. Mama had people over and showed it in our living room, with cookies and Coca-Cola. Neighbors, church members, business friends of my father's, came and saw the light. And this is the point: in my home town, in my circle of friends, just about nobody smokes. Middle-aged men still come up to me and tell how my mother scared hell out of them when they were twelve.

The press loved her. We must have four scrapbooks, five, filled with clippings: Mama making her hole-in-one, Mama winning State, Mama refusing to let the electric company mutilate our street's trees, Mama taking a deep breath. She's got this big toothy smile and a poster tan; she looks like a lady who plays dirty if she has to. She's also got these big double-dipper breasts (they got in the way of her backswing, she said) and legs that didn't stop: it was no fun having boys come home from college and watching them fall all over themselves—for Mama. Was I jealous? Sure I was. But mostly I wanted some of that zip for myself.

Somehow—and chiefly by accident, but that's another story—after graduation I got a job on an island. Merritt Island, Florida. It was the jumping-off place for the world, the Cape: Grissom and Glenn, Saturn and Mercury, Atlas, Titan, the Original Seven. And I was there, a reporter, albeit the lowest, the worst paid, the most questionably qualified, impatiently tolerated, and condescended-to reporter on the staff of *Today*. The education staffer in a town obsessed with space. ("What's an IQ?" my editor asked. "A number," I said. He liked that, and I had the job.) He thought I had the stuff, and I had to believe him: it was my life he was talking about. He was the editor of the best newsweekly in the United States: *Time*, that unimpeachable source, had said so. It was a good place to be in the sixties, and I had fallen into it. And it was one thousand miles from home.

"This can't be good," Daddy said.

"Go to it," Mama said.

The morning I left their house, the sun glinted off the gravel in the driveway; I sat in my new blue Falcon, the back seat full of clothes, books, Joan Baez albums. My father, still in his robe and needing a shave, stood in the driveway beside the car. He kept cleaning his already spotless glasses with a paper towel, standing in one spot and not saying much.

Mama kept asking, "Are you sure you haven't forgotten anything?" and "Promise you won't drive if you feel tired. Call us as soon as you stop tonight."

"Call collect." My father gave me four fifties, which, added to what he had already given me for the trip, amounted to more than my first month's salary.

"I don't need this much."

"She's right," Mama said. "Let her manage. She'll call us if she needs anything. You think she's going to forget the number?"

"Just in case," Daddy said. "You never know what might happen."

I put the fifties in my purse.

"I don't want you breaking down on the highway," he said, although he had bought my new car expressly to prevent that.

I leaned my cheek against my father's and felt the early-morning stubble. It surprised me, that, and the fact that I was nearly as tall as he.

Mama remembered something and zoomed back inside the house.

"I've got to *go*," I said. I wanted to make five hundred miles a day and it was already a half-hour past sunrise.

Mama reached in the car and put six—six! bananas and two peaches in a plastic bag on the front seat. "Don't forget to call," she said, holding my father's hand.

"All right. All right!" From the end of the driveway I shouted, "I'll call you tonight!" and then I pulled onto Letitia Street, headed for highways south and southeast. The prospect of being paid to write stretched in front of me like the miles; I had wanted to be a writer since fourth-grade Mrs. Weeks had read my essays aloud to the sixth-grade class. The sun was at the corner of Letitia and Belmont streets; by the time it set I would be in Tallahassee. Mississippi, Alabama, and Georgia rolled past; the Gulf coast, with its trees all bent in from the ocean; then the red dirt hills. All of it seemed clean, autumnal, new as print. I rolled down the windows of the Falcon and sang along with the radio, loud as I could. The songs stayed the same while the announcers' accents flattened out. By the time I got to Florida's Highway A1A, all my bananas were gone.

When I arrived at Merritt Island, I drove straight through town to an isolated part of the beach. I climbed over the dunes that separated A1A from the ocean, past the whine of the highway's cars, past the black ribbons of seaweed strung at the high tide line. I squinted; the wind that always blows in from the Atlantic was blowing for the first time in my face. The wind smelled like ocean. I took off my loafers and socks and walked out on the hard coarse surface of the wet sand. To my left, the gantries of Cape Kennedy blurred in the humidity; right, the beach trailed and shimmered like a long white scarf. A foolish wave, colder than I expected, rolled to my feet, paused, and retreated. Sandpipers chased the foam, peeping and searching for food. They left, I noticed, three-pointed tracks, like stars with the bottoms cut off.

"Ponce de Leon!" I hollered to the gulls. "Balboa!"

My river-bound Louisiana soul unbuckled like the waves. I splashed into the Atlantic, not even rolling up my doubleknits. I was twenty-one; I had a job on the best newsweekly in the country; I was inventing myself for real.

It lasted two weeks.

And then my father died.

A few days after the funeral, when it was time to reopen the store for business, Mr. Brant, our office manager, called from the U-Tote-M across the street.

"Would you try to find your father's keys to the store?" he asked me. "I hate to bother you, you know? But we can't get in the back warehouse."

"What?" Mama came to the phone, assuming it was for her. "The keys?" She had deep circles around her eyes, like bruises. "Where would they be? The keys, the keys . . ."

My Aunt Adele was making coffee in the kitchen and she said to me, "What about the pants your father was wearing?"

Mrs. Morgan, our next-door neighbor, said, "Wouldn't you think those people would take care of that and not bother Virginia?"

"There was a package the ambulance left," I said. "A paper sack with things in it."

"Well, there," Adele said.

Mama and I found the keys in the sack, drove over, and opened the back warehouse. I'm not sure my mother had ever been inside; I'm sure I hadn't. It was crammed with merchandise: Italian cane-back chairs, mattresses, Sealy, Beautyrest, DreamCloud, tables, credenzas, breakfronts; Trouvailles, Sligh, Baker. Hotpoint appliances, Zenith electronics. Most of it wasn't unpacked; it was still in crates or shrink wraps. Here was thousands of dollars worth of merchandise, most of it not paid for, though we didn't know that yet. Mr. Brant flicked on the switch with his knuckle and thanked us for coming over. He was a smiling man, a good salesman who remembered people's names. My father had liked him. But today Mr. Brant looked like a man who was afraid he was going to lose his job.

"You don't worry about a thing, Mrs. D.," he said. "We've got the inventory. We're going to keep everything ship-shape, just like Mr. D. would have wanted."

"I know you will," Mama said. "We appreciate that, Mr. Brant."

"Do you"—Mr. Brant looked somewhat embarrassed—"want to let us know what to do about the safe?"

"What's wrong with it?"

"Can't open it, Mrs. D. Don't have the combination."

And my mother, who could drive a wood off the men's tee with the best golfers in the club, who could put a wing on the Children's Hospital practically singlehanded, didn't even know the combination to my father's safe.

"Sell the business," advised my aunt, who was dying to know how much my father had left us, and eager to offer consolation provided the amount was not too much. "Sell! You don't need the trouble."

"I'm not sure what I'm going to do," Mama said. "I think Mollie and I could handle it."

"You've got inflation," Adele said. "You've got bills. You've got long hours. You've got no-good salesmen." She recited woe like a Greek chorus. "What do you know about sales? What do you know about accounting? What do you know, Virginia?"

"I don't know anything," my mother admitted. "But I know I don't want to talk about all this right now."

That week people came over, day after day, night after night. Adele, my Uncle Peter, their kids, Joyce and Petey. Also the couples my parents had played bridge with for twenty years. Also neighbors. They ate food that they brought and they talked to my mother, trying to cheer her up or at least distract her. To a certain extent, it worked— we had beers, we talked—but eventually everybody left and my mother and I were alone in the house. She let in Lady, the dog, who had always slept outside. Lady curled up at the foot of Mama's bed as though she had slept there every night of her life.

"You know something?" Mama said, standing there in her pink bathrobe, brushing her teeth. "I've always shared a room. My sister and I slept together until I got married. Then Arthur. I've never slept by myself. I'm afraid I can't."

She had certainly slept alone—my father had traveled to the furniture markets twice a year—but it wasn't the time to remind her. Instead I pulled on my nightgown and climbed into my parents' double bed, on the side where my father had slept less than a week before. I piled the pillows together and leaned back against the headboard while she stayed in the bathroom, brushing.

"When are you going back?" she called to me.

"I told them I'd stay a week." She didn't say anything right away so I added, "I can stay longer if you need me. I told them at least a week."

"That's good," she said. "I'm glad of that." She came back in the bedroom and said, "Tell me what it's like. The people you work with." She unscrewed a jar of Eterna 27 and smoothed it around her eyes with delicate upward sweeps of her middle finger.

"They're OK. We work all the time, seven o'clock every night. Sometimes later. Last Friday I was at the office until two in the morning."

"Why so late?"

"It takes me twice as long as anybody else. But I'm catching on." She made an ambiguous *hmm* through closed lips, possibly disapproving my tardiness, possibly incredulous that I wasn't already surpassing all others.

"They're helpful," I said. "Really smart, too."

"Let me tell you something. Your father was sending you money, twice. He gave it to me, to send to you. You didn't get it because I didn't send it. That was my idea, to let you live on your salary, but I didn't tell him. He wanted you to have more." She wasn't apologizing, just setting forth facts. "I should have sent it."

"I didn't need it. I don't want it."

"I know, but your father wanted you to have it." She looked at me in a way that signaled the end of the subject. "Did you know that when I went to tournaments, he'd pack my bags?"

"No, I didn't."

"To make sure I hadn't forgotten anything. Even my clubs."

"Would you have forgotten them?"

"Maybe." She tried to smile, but it didn't quite come off. "Who knows?"

They had been happy; when I was growing up, I thought all married people were happy. They had loved to go out. Mama would step out of the bath, fragrant and wet; she'd open the bathroom door to let out the steam. Her skin was tanned darker than her hair, and the white outline of her golf shorts and shirt made her seem twice vulnerable.

The dress she would wear hung in the closet. Her evening clothes cost hundreds of dollars, even in the fifties, but my father loved the way she dressed. She would be fastening her merry widow and he would offer to help with all the little hooks. Then he'd slip his hands inside the cups. I, trespassing, was all eyes. Mama bounced away: "You'd better watch it," she said. "I love to watch it," he answered. She laughed; then he went off looking for his studs, looking tickled with himself.

When my mother was zipped, humid, teak-colored, and fragrant, and she and my father had left for their dance, I locked the door against the babysitter and stepped into a green satin dress Mama had decided against wearing. I pulled up the neckline—it flapped against my ten-year-old chest like a lowered mainsail—and hitched up the top with a safety pin. I hung my mother's pearls around my neck, dangled rhinestones from my ears. Then I dotted on enough perfume to drive the cat under the bed. I found my mother's green slippers, stiletto-heeled, and flopped over to the full-length mirror to admire.

That's when the babysitter knocked on the door. "Time to go to bed," she said.

On the Friday before I was going to leave, my Aunt Adele came into my room while I was writing a letter. She closed the door and began talking in a low voice. My mother was on the other side of the house, in the kitchen.

"Mollie," Adele said, "I don't think it's a good idea for you to leave. Not right now."

"You mean stay another week?"

"No. Another six months. Maybe a year."

The suggestion seemed so impossible that I just stared at her for a minute.

"Virginia's scared to death," she continued, "but don't expect her to admit it."

"I can't stay that long. I have a job. They expect me to come back."

"They'd certainly understand if you didn't."

"They would, but I couldn't get that kind of job here."

"Does that matter so much?"

"It matters a lot."

"More than your mother?"

"Of course not!" I said, but Adele wasn't going to be interrupted.

"If you stayed with her for a while—who's saying forever?—she'd adjust better. And you could always go back to your job later."

"They wouldn't keep it open six months."

"Have you asked them?"

She knew, of course, in the way that people who ask rhetorical questions always know, that I hadn't.

Adele put her hand on my shoulder and regarded me with expectation. "Your mother's deceptive," she said. "She looks like she can do anything. But when it comes to the real business of the world, she doesn't know a damned thing. You've had four years of college, a job. You could help her right now, and she needs you. Don't you know that?"

"No," I answered. "And I think you're wrong about what she can do."

After she closed the door I stared at the letter I had been writing until I could no longer see it. That my aunt was a meddling guiltmonger, serving it right up front like mother's milk, I had no doubt. She would have cheerfully admitted it herself. But that she could also be right!—and this was where the nerve met the burn—that was unthinkable. I think I hated Adele at that moment. She had seen the way I looked; she must have known how I felt. And she expected to win; her last shot was, "You see? You know the right thing to do." The tears in my eyes were her claim to victory. I couldn't answer her—I don't think I could answer even now. But I knew one thing: on Monday I was going back to work.

Saturday morning, five people were in the house. Adele and Mrs. Morgan were in the den watching a re-run of *Garden Time:* how to grow ageratum, begonias, petunias, and shamrocks from seed. In their Sears-bright slacks and sweater sets, they looked like petunias gone to seed themselves. Claire, our old housekeeper who had retired when her arthritis got too bad, was back; her outsized knuckles, whorled like tree nodes, gripped the handle of an Electrolux. The monotonous whirr of the vacuum held its own with *Garden Time*. In the kitchen I was watching my mother fix lunch. She was slicing purple onions for a salad.

"Want some help?" I asked.

"How about a glass of sherry? You two want some sherry?" she called into the den.

"We'll get it."

"Sit tight," Mama commanded. "Mollie will bring it."

In the refrigerator were remnants of quiche and a ham casserole still left over from the wake, also two bottles of Harvey's. One bottle was almost empty, so I took both out.

"You drank all this?" I asked my mother.

"Last night, so I could sleep. Open the other."

"The doctor advised it, instead of sleeping pills," Adele called from the den.

"Well, that's too much," I said in a lower voice. I brought two glasses into the den, where a woman in high heels was showing the home gardener how to transplant seedlings that have been sprouted in egg cartons. "I can't hear the program in the kitchen," I told Adele. "Mind if I turn it up?" That fixed the eavesdropping.

"Take it easy," I told my mother back in the kitchen.

"I can't sleep. I'll pour it myself if it worries you so much."

"I'm not worried."

"I just can't sleep, is all."

I knew that: all night I could feel her throwing back the covers, covering up again; I heard her crying. I wasn't sleeping either; twice the night before I was wakened by a dream: I was back in Cocoa Beach, on the island, a narrow spit of land two blocks wide, between mainland and ocean. A storm approached, black cumulus clouds rolling in from the east. I was looking for my father, who was in one of the island's vacation houses. All the houses were on stilts. Rain began to fall—there was real rain outside, driving against the window—and water began to rise on the island. It covered the beach, the dunes, the highway. By the time I realized I needed to leave, it was too late: the bridge was down. The second time I woke up, I went downstairs in the dark, my bare feet freezing on the linoleum. I sat at the kitchen table, unable to stop crying or to shake off the dream. I wanted to tell Mama. Finally I went back to bed, and just before dawn, I fell asleep.

"What are we having?" I asked her now.

I lifted the lid of one of the pots on the stove. Inside were pole beans, lying on top of the collapsible steel colander that she had steamed them in. I upended the lid like a shield to keep the steam from burning my hand.

"You can turn that off," Mama said. "They're ready."

I poured Bristol Cream into two stemmed glasses and set one on the counter beside my mother. She had finished with the purple onions and now she was tearing spinach leaves from their stems. Her hands moved quickly, and her work produced a moist and rhythmic sound. Her back was toward me, her head inclined slightly forward. She was standing, it seemed to me, as she had stood for the last twenty years, fixing oatmeal or coffee or the vegetables that she bought early in the mornings from the old man who used to peddle produce from a three-wheeled bicycle cart. He'd come down the street ringing his bell, often during breakfast; my mother and I would stop in the middle of oatmeal and rush out before he passed our house. The fruits and vegetables rested in slatted wooden crates on the bed of the cart. Mama showed me how to select pole beans; mottled or solid green, it didn't matter. Get them the same circumference, that way they cook evenly. Get them small, about one-quarter-inch diameter; they're younger, tenderer. She'd snap one: I learned to listen for the pop. I learned how to look at things from my mother.

"Richard thinks we should incorporate," she was saying in a voice beneath the television's cover. Her back was toward me, her hands were methodically tearing spinach leaves. "He thinks we could find a good manager. Maybe Mr. Brant would work out."

"Sure he would. But Mama, you don't need a lawyer to tell you that."

"You think." She looked up. "You think."

"If you can organize the women's golf association, you can run a business."

"Isn't that a little naive?" Her voice when she spoke was flat. "I never walked in that office except to draw out money." She shook her head. "And these success stories . . . did you ever notice? They're all about young women. I'm forty-nine years old." She seemed to have finished, then added, "One thing, Richard's right. We should incorporate. To protect us against debts."

"We have debts?"

"Yes, some. Not big ones. Not too big. The insurance . . . it's . . . I don't know what all these papers mean! What to sign, what to keep . . ." She loosed an audible breath across the kitchen. "You ought to look at them before you leave. I'll ask Richard to hurry it up. Could you stay for that?"

"Monday. Could we do it Monday?"

"I'll call and ask."

She finished with the spinach and tossed the salad in its mahogany bowl, the dark wrinkled leaves green against the purple onions. "There," she said, turning around to face me. "Doesn't that look pretty?"

I stayed at home five more days; the incorporation papers weren't ready until Wednesday afternoon. When my mother and I drove back from the attorney's office, my bags were in the back seat. We drove past supermarkets, past shopping centers with parking lots like grey lakes, out of the city, toward the airport. It was humidly cold, and the tires rotated against the pavement with a monotonous, heart-like beat. Mama leaned toward the steering wheel.

"I think Richard is overcharging us," she said. "Did you see the bill he gave me?" Without taking her eyes off the road, she rummaged in her purse and gave me a cleanly typed sheet with an engraved letterhead. "He's so afraid he won't get his money, he didn't even wait to mail it to me."

"Legal services," I read out loud. "$450." I looked up. It shocked me, too, but then I had never had bills of any kind. "That must be for the incorporation." I kept reading. "Telephone consultation, October 8, $15. October 11, $15." There were two other telephone consultations.

"Mama," I said, "don't call him so much."

My mother stepped on the gas and pulled around a car in front of us. "I had to call him. What do you want me to do?" Her voice dropped, a sure sign that she was angry. "How much did your father ever tell me? Mollie, I can't do all this by myself!"

"Maybe I can do something."

She rammed the bill back into her purse. "It's pretty hard to do anything when you're five states away."

There we were.

She concentrated, frowning, on her driving, and stared at the painted stripes on the highway. I listened to the tires thump the cracks in the pavement. It was a long drive to the airport.

When she and I had driven my father to the train station for one of his buying trips, Mama had always taken
his leaving hard, no matter how many times he had gone
before, no matter if the trip lasted only a week. We'd all
wait for the train, Daddy looking good in a Burberry coat
bought especially for the trip. It would be cold, but none of
us wanted to wait inside the tobacco-dense depot. My parents stood on the platform holding hands while I sat on my
father's Samsonite two-suiter to ask, "How many minutes
now?" Mama, every time, gave me the answer. When the
train pulled up, all black steel and vibrations, massive loud
threatening metal, my father embraced my mother, holding
her head in his big hands, his fingers in her pale hair. Then
he reached down and lifted me so that we were all eye to eye.

"Mind your mother," he said, "and I'll bring you something from Chicago."

"What?" I asked. "What what what?"

"Hush," Mama said. "Your father's leaving now."

I looked at her in surprise. Her eyes were wet, and my
father hadn't even boarded yet.

"Goodbye, Arthur," she said. "Goodbye, Sweetheart!"
Her tears left a spot on the lapel of his new coat.

The memory caught me like the sight of his razor in
the bathroom.

The airport waiting room was overheated. Outside,
wind scattered occasional flurries of rain. The airplane

attendants wore yellow slickers that were reflected in the blacktop's shine. In Cocoa Beach people would be walking the beaches in their bathing suits, but here, in this room, it was winter.

"I'm thinking," Mama said as we took adjoining seats, "that maybe I ought to rent out the house. Get an apartment."

"An apartment? Where?"

"Where Crissy Owens lives, maybe? She told me there's one available in her building."

"Would you like that?" I didn't like to think of my mother without trees and a gravel driveway out front.

"Who says I wouldn't? I'd be fine."

"What about our furniture?"

"Sell it. Or store it. I don't need such a big place."

"Who'd you rent to?"

"I'd find somebody good. It would be income." She smiled in a way meant to be reassuring. "Not that we have to worry so much." I half-expected her to reach in her purse and pull out a half-dozen bananas.

"No," she repeated. "We don't have to worry so much."

"I'm not worried." The loudspeaker announced my flight, first call. "I just don't think you should rush into anything. Richard said not to rush into anything."

People rose from their seats and scooped up packages. Some began to line up: little boys in white sneakers, caught in the vise–like grip of their mothers; businessmen with leather envelopes; old ladies in mink stoles. Neither my mother nor I moved.

"I'll be home before Christmas," I said. "We can talk about it then, if you want."

"I'm not sure I want to wait until Christmas."

"Then I'll call as soon as I get home."

Home.

I tilted my head to kiss my mother; then I leaned down and hugged her. Did I feel my mother tremble? More likely it was myself.

The other passengers disappeared into the plane's jet-way. Up close, my mother's perfume surrounded me like the green memory of a dress.

"Mama," I said as the attendant waited for the ticket. "You know I want to stay, don't you?"

"Oh, Mollie. Can't you come back? Go, and come back?"

Behind her, the attendant looked at her watch.

I knew that whatever I said, it wouldn't be right.

"I'll call you when I get there," I repeated finally. "You'll be OK, Mama, I know you will."

She gave me a look that said it: *I don't know.*

She didn't know.

ATALANTA'S LOVER

$\mathcal{M}$el is a runner. He disdains joggers. He scorns their puny gastrocs, their flabby quadriceps, their blue acrylic Saks jogging suits with the yellow side racing stripes. Snow in January, slippery leaves in October, Aztec sun in August do not flag him, no fair-weather fleet-foot.

Mel is doing warmup exercises on the grassy sidelines of the parking lot near the east end of the Memorial-Allen Parkway bike trail, a beautiful trail with the highest hills, trees, muggers, and carbon monoxide level in the city. Up, down. Up, down. Inhale, *two, three*. Exhale, *five, six*. Mel stretches. See him stretch, his biceps femoris stringy and lean, his tendons supple as the leather upholstery of his Mustang Shelby GT 350. Out, press. Observe him well: his feet, encased in $385 Airgliders made to order from 3-D printouts of Mel's feet; his calves, 16 ¼ inches around at rest, fully 16 ½ after his run; his knees, their cartilage already

63

compacting, their patellas protruding nakedly. Notice the discreet bulge on the lower left side of his all-cotton shorts, of his wondrous machine nestled snugly within the protective mesh cradle of his $12 All-America Giant-Killer athletic supporter, on sale at selected stores for $6.95 in green, red, paisley, and shocking cream. His waist, taut. His stomach, flat on the *five, six*; protruding correctly on the *two, three*. His chest, if not precisely convex, nor even remotely suggestive of Hercules's, at least respectable. A man Aristotle himself would respect.

Now Mel begins, first depressing the black chrome timer release of his shock-resistant Rolex Maritimer digital chronometer that reads to the tenth of a second, both local and Greenwich time, while also giving the date, temperature, position of the earth at perihelion, and location of the only good all-night deli in Houston. Red digits march across the surface, smooth as Mel's brow. Zoom, he's off!

> Heel, toe, heel, toe
> Away we go.

The first mile, the second mile, fall away as easily as sweat. Mel now enters the meaningful Alpha rhythm, arms loose (bent slightly more than 90 degrees), shoulders down, neck lifted (but not too much). Joggers (inferior beings), pitiable overweight hausfraus in tennis shoes, middle-aged men windedly defying coronary, are passed like so much chaff by this whirlwind. Mel goes a little faster here near the street, where passersby can admire.

But wait! What is this? Mel is passed—*passed!*—by no ordinary jogger but by an extraordinary female form, two perfectly shaped oval glutei maximi pumping past him covered by the thinnest of—it must be admitted—blue acrylic Saks yellow-striped jogging shorts, provocatively slit up the sides and surely—surely!—covered by no other garment underneath. Mel swings wide to the left in an effort to obtain a better glimpse. Her face, what he can see of it, seems strangely familiar.

Already Mel knows that they must meet. How? He strains mightily to keep up. She glances over her left shoulder. His breath comes in hot gasps. She does not smile, she looks alarmed! What a stupe he is; he must not be so obvious! She may think he is a mugger, or the jogging rapist (for he has read of one such athletic but demented soul). She presses forward at a quickened pace, leaving him bereft and winded, her delectable mystery, her strangely familiar features, disappearing around a bend of the trail, perhaps forever.

Days pass. Mel arrives at his usual hour, punctual as a bridegroom, but She is not seen again. A week passes. He no longer strains ahead or looks behind as he chalks up his miles (inhale, *two, three*; exhale, *five, six*); She is gone. Another week: it rains. The skies fill with water, pools gather on the ground, jogging trails slither in mud. Mel takes to the streets, where he is sprayed by passing cars and challenged by yardbound beagles. No matter. He trains, he trains.

Then the sun comes out; the water runs off; the whole world comes out to jog. As Mel parks his 350 in the Memorial-Allen Parkway lot, he sees her, there on the grassy side plot, warming up.

"Excuse me," he says, "but didn't we meet several weeks ago in the Athlete's Foot? You were being fitted for some custom orthotics?"

"Try it again, buster." Solid ice. "I get my inserts from a specialist in Dallas. Practice limited to runners."

"In the Safeway, in front of the Dr. Scholl's display?"

She does not answer. Instead she begins a graceful series of squats.

Desperate, Mel decides to make a clean breast of things. "I've seen you run," he says, "and the way your sartorius ripples across your vastus . . . well, it's beautiful."

She listens, but she doesn't miss a squat.

"How far do you go?" he asks, getting right to the point.

"I'm not into distance." Contempt. "I do two miles in nine and a half minutes."

A few days later, over herbal tea and sprouted kidney beans at the Hobbit Hole, she tells him the story of her life. She was an orphan, raised by kindly bears in the Austin hill country. Not only can she run; she reads everything, forgets nothing; she speaks fluent Ursus; and she makes the best liquified liver eggnog in town. Mel is in love at once, but she isn't interested. "I would never," she tells him, "consider marrying any man I could beat in a foot race." Mel considers, and despairs. What chance has he, a mere mortal (blessed though he is with excellent teeth, a bear-like hairiness, and perfect arches) to win this goddess Atalanta?

She would have spent the rest of her life happily living among the bears, had not a roving advertising man spotted her one day and asked her to pose for an anti-smoking campaign. That was where Mel had seen her: on page one of a two-page commentary in *Time* she was the housewife carelessly tossing a lighted match into her kitchen trash bin. Turn the page, and all of her children are burning up, not to mention dinner. Thirteen people had written to say they would never burn down their kitchens again. Four billionaires from Texas proposed. The U.S. Fire Administration Marshal sent her a self-extinguishing ashcan. None of it turned her head. She remained a simple goddess, though she bought a River Oaks highrise and read Saint-Simon and Kant in the afternoons.

If she has a weakness, Mel thinks, it is reading. She loves to read, devouring the messages on the backs of cereal boxes along with the whole grains inside, finishing the complete works of Elias Ashmole, never skipping a word about the author or the typeface at the ends of novels. She cannot even throw away lengthy letters beginning, "Only you can save the Houston toad from extinction . . ." She reads to the end and sometimes sends money. It is clear she can resist nothing in print. Mel considers disguising himself as the *OED* and mailing himself to her.

He ponders the meaning of their relationship. It's only physical, he thinks, but what else is there? Then he recalls a line she sometimes quotes: "The head Sublime, the heart Pathos, the genitals Beauty, the hands and feet Proportion." Not, then, all physical? He must learn to run faster—but also to use his head.

Day by day Mel runs, no longer on the Memorial-Allen Parkway trail, but now at the Rice University track, keeping a watchful eye on his sweep-second Rolex. His joints ache. His knees creak. His tendons, shins, feet, groin, and cardio-vascular system rebel. Even his arches let him down. There is such a thing, his sources advise, as running through the pain. And what pain greater than the sure loss of the fairest runner of them all?

Later she meets him at his apartment, bearing BenGay and a complete, annotated guide to *Runners' World*. They have returned from a two-mile run (she in 9:22.14; he in 13:47.9) and are drinking Mel's newly-purchased angelica seed tea. How fair the beloved looks, flushed from her exertions! Mel gazes, distracted between her beauty and his desire for a teaspoonful of pernicious white sugar in the revolting tea. He wants very badly to talk with her but she is engrossed in reading the essay on the back of the box of loose (bulk pack) tea leaves.

"I've got to go," she says, draining her cup to the last angelica seed.

"Wait!" Mel cries. "We can't go on, having tea like this. I need a pastrami sandwich. I want a chicken-fried steak."

"'All wholesome food is caught without a net or a trap.' Of what can you be thinking?"

He is insane with anguish, longing, low blood sugar. "I'll give up eating entirely," he promises, "if only you'll marry me."

"You've got to beat me in a race. You know this story."

"Tomorrow morning at six?"

"As you wish."

What madness is this? He knows he cannot win. Her time has always been better than his. His legs ache from continual punishment. He never gets up before eight. He must use his head, not his heels. A plan, a plan!

Six o'clock comes, an hour no mortal should have to know exists. Brutal darkness. Mel is at the starting line.

She arrives, lovely in her blue acrylic Saks yellow-striped running shorts (with the provocative side slit). Mel aches at the sight of her.

"On your mark."

"Get set."

"GO!"

They are off. By straining his mightiest, he keeps abreast of her for the first hundred yards. His feet lift; his lungs are inspired; he is swift, powerful, almost a god himself... but no: nearly imperceptibly, she draws shoulder to shoulder with him; then she inches ahead; and he is behind her once again. It is time!

Suddenly, out of the morning dark, almost directly in front of his beloved, an electronic message board flashes on, a slowly scrolling billboard with hundreds of tiny LEDs spelling these words: REDUCE SPEED. She cannot miss it. But is it enough? Will she break stride for it? Mel's heart, thundering, nearly bursts. She does slow down—or has he imagined it? Yes, she takes it in! It is enough. Mel regains his place beside her.

Again they compete, again the fleet one takes the lead. All seems lost, but no! Miraculously, a second distraction appears, this one a little to the side, obliquely placed, more dimly lit.

DEAREST (for so the second sign reads), I LOVE YOU. I HAVE GIVEN UP SAUSAGE AND HASHED BROWNS FOR YOU. That is all. Is it enough? To read it, she will have to swerve slightly.

She does! He gains the lead, but only momentarily; again, she is in front, her thighs thrusting away from his forever.

The last golden marquee (cunningly placed far wide of the track) gleams now through the morning mist. It is 25 words long, and set in the center, like a precious ingot, is an ingeniously ambiguous word designed to stop her cold:

MOST ADORABLE ONE, WE WILL BE HAPPY TOGETHER. WE WILL RUN THROUGH THE TRAILS OF LIFE IF YOU WILL ALLOW IT. WE WILL RAISE LITTLE BEARS TOGETHER. MARRY ME.

MEL

As her eyes widen (trails? trials?), her lover, damp, winded, victorious, crosses the finish line. She is his.

Some say they were turned into lions (literary) and were seen regularly on 4:00 a.m. Book TV. Others tell (and this is more to be believed) that, assisted by Cupid, they negotiated a marriage contract and ascended to Mount Olympus, to live as myth forever.

MATTHEW

$\mathcal{M}$ost of the time Margaret was serene; unflappable, her husband said. Married not quite four months to the man she loved, she was happier than she sometimes felt anyone had a right to be. On this particular Thursday evening, however, with Ray in Atlanta on a business trip while she stayed at home with his son Matthew, she was edgy.

She was fixing chili for supper. Matthew, keeping his stepmother company in the kitchen (while she heartily wished he wouldn't), said, "This is great. Why don't we ever have chili when Dad's home?"

"There's going to be a salad, too."

"That's OK," Matthew agreed. "As long as I don't have to eat tomatoes."

Margaret was offended. "You don't have to eat them," she explained with more sharpness in her voice than she wished. "But when somebody fixes you something, you shouldn't complain about it."

"All right, all right." Matthew had his eight-year-old antennae up. "You want to play guns after supper? You can use my Air Blaster."

"You've got a violin lesson. Mrs. Leopardi's coming, remember?"

"After that? Just one game?"

"No."

"Please?" Matthew moved from the sink area to a spot more directly in Margaret's way. "One game after the violin lesson? I'll show you the rules."

"I'm tired, Matt," Margaret said. What she wanted was to go lie down with a glass of wine. "Not tonight." She hadn't realized how much Ray did at home until his trip to Atlanta, his first time away since they were married. Today, she had left her office early, at four thirty, so she could pick Matthew up from his after-school day care and deliver him to Scouts by five fifteen. Her division manager—Margaret did research for environmental consultants—didn't seem to mind, but there was a meeting late in the day that she hadn't been able to attend. After the meeting the staff usually went somewhere for a drink, and Margaret had missed that, too. While Matthew was at Boy Scouts, she beat her way to a Safeway store, where she picked up milk, lettuce, whole-wheat bread, and chili, a few things that Matthew would eat without making a fuss. By the time she returned to the Boy Scouts, through traffic that was now nearly immobilized (a car had stalled in the left lane, turning a two-mile trip into a forty-five minute ordeal), she barely had time left to get Matt home and start dinner before Mrs. Leopardi arrived at seven. Margaret had been up since six. It seemed that her day had been a timed race, a sprint from one appointment to the next. She felt over-caffeinated and smaller of breath, pushed in on all sides.

She lifted the lid on the red enameled pot of chili, Hormel's Ranch Style, No Beans. Spooned over franks onto untoasted buns, chili was going to be supper. Cumin spice warmed the air.

"Houston, we have reached boil. Repeat, we have reached boil," said Matthew, marching stiff-legged around the table like the walking robot he and his dad had made. Margaret, feeling more authentically mechanical, put plates, forks, and two glasses of milk on the table. Four copies of *Bon Appetit* magazine, one for each month of her marriage, lay stacked on an open shelf. This meal wasn't, Margaret thought, what *Bon Appetit* had in mind. She had forgotten to set out napkins, but decided to skip them.

"Chili is neat-o," Matthew said, leaving a red trail of grease between the main dish and his plate. "I wish we could have it all the time."

Margaret ignored this information. Matthew would eat nothing but meat and bread seven days a week if she let him. He disliked milk, all green vegetables, most fruits, anything in a casserole, and even unfamiliar desserts. Before her marriage, Margaret had loved to cook a special meal; but now she found mealtimes a chore. If she fixed what she and Ray liked, Matthew literally choked; if she fixed only what Matthew liked, they'd all have rickets.

"So," she asked, studying the grease as it oozed into the wood of the table, "what did you do today?"

"We made up this game," Matthew said. "With a pair of dice. You set up two deals and roll the dice to get the answer, see? Like if somebody's chasing you and you come to a high cliff. If you roll one to six, you have to jump over the ledge. Seven to twelve, you stay and fight. Let's say I have to jump the cliff. I get to roll next, and one to six, I swim away in the river that's at the bottom. Seven to twelve, I break my arm and he comes after me. You make up stuff as you go along, see."

"I see," said Margaret, "but none of those alternatives seems very attractive to me."

"It's fun," Matthew insisted. "You want to play it sometime?" He poured out a lengthy description of hypothetical violence, miraculous detections followed by equally miraculous escapes. Margaret tuned out: she had no sympathy with rocks and hard places, children's games. Her brothers—she had four, all younger than herself—used to play such games when they were children, and she had found no use for them even then. Margaret still wore a scar in the center of her forehead from a tomahawk launched too accurately by one of her brothers, an over-zealous Apache, when she was twelve.

"So what else?" she asked when Matthew took a breath. "What did you do in school?"

"Nothing."

"Nothing? You sat and stared?"

"Well, a man came from the deaf school," Matthew said. "He showed us sign language." He held up his right forefinger and laid it against his lips. "You know what this means?"

"What?"

"Shhh!" Matthew whispered. "It means *quiet*."

"That's a good one." Margaret made the sign. "What else?"

Matthew pointed to himself. "*I*."

"*I*."

He pointed to her. "*You*." Then he spread his thumb and forefinger into an L shape. "What's this?"

"Beats me."

Matthew made a circle with his fingers and thumb.

"Zero!"

"Nope." He held two fingers in a V, like Churchill.

"Victory?"

"No." He made a partially-opened fist, with the back of his hand straight but the fingers right-angled downward at the first knuckle. "This one's tough," Matthew admitted.

"I give up. Tell me."

"You can't give up. You've got to guess."

"Matthew," Margaret said, wishing she had her glass of pinot noir that very minute, "I can't guess. I guessed already and I was wrong. It looks very mysterious to me."

Matthew sounded exasperated. "It spells a word. Like"—he spelled out the word with his small greasy hands—"I L-O-V-E chili."

"I see. Eat your salad. What else did you learn?"

"That's it," Matthew said. "I can't remember everything."

By closing the doors to the living room, the hall, and the bedroom, Margaret could effectively shut out most of the sound of the violin lesson. Honoring her promise to herself, she poured exactly five ounces of wine into a stemmed glass and ran a little tap water into the glass to make it go further. Then she carried it into the bedroom. She would have liked a square of chocolate, but she didn't want to risk going back to the kitchen; Mrs. Leopardi might decide to ask why Matthew hadn't been practicing again. In the past, Mrs. Leopardi had hinted darkly that she wouldn't put up forever with a pupil who didn't touch the violin once between lessons. Mrs. Leopardi had an artist's soul; she had studied at the Curtis; she had an "I ♥ Mahler" sticker on her violin case.

Margaret, stretching out on the bed, the pinot noir now warming her throat, closed her eyes in a moment of empathy with Mrs. Leopardi. "*Agitato!*" Margaret could hear the teacher imploring through three closed doors. "*Agitato!* Like this . . . No!"

Matthew had been practicing this piece since January of last year. Margaret had heard it, she once estimated, 120 times since she met Ray, but not often enough, apparently. She was tired of encouraging Matthew to practice, and his father's efforts, though earnest, were sporadic. "How long has he been taking lessons?" she asked Ray shortly after the wedding. "Four years? And he still doesn't play with vibrato?"

"It's hard to play the violin," Ray had answered, "and I just want him to like good music when he grows up. He doesn't have to be a professional musician."

Matthew, in no danger of becoming a professional musician, did seem to quite enjoy the lessons, especially when Mrs. Leopardi remembered how badly she needed students and was nicer to him. "A dilettante," Margaret told herself. "That's what we're rearing."

Against her better judgment she poured herself two more ounces of wine and opened her eyes. The tortured chromatics of the "Valse Triste" filtered in with a certain skewed harmony. It took twenty-one years to develop a fully grown person, to hammer the ignorant, self-seeking primitive child into some kind of responsible adult. Matthew was not yet halfway there. Nothing was wrong with him that a dozen years would not improve. She could not have reared a better child herself, and she knew it.

The thing was, she wouldn't have reared any child herself. She resented the incursions into her time, and she had serious work ambitions. She had been barely pubescent, helping her mother raise four boys, when she had seen through the myth of mellow motherhood. What a fraud! How had childbearing gotten its good reputation? Like anything else that needed a heavy propaganda, the product must be intrinsically deficient. Yet here she was with Matthew—because Ray, the one man in her life that she had absolutely wanted to marry, was a single father. "Two men for the price of one," she had joked at their wedding reception. But she had managed to love only Ray.

As a young woman, years before she married, Margaret had had a dream: she was at a reception for a bride and groom. The married pair sat on a raised platform at a long table; they were in the center, flanked by beautiful children and wedding guests. Margaret sat at another table, watching. The bride had been young and gracious, the groom erotic and rich, and Margaret had envied them. She felt hurt, neglected, at being put at a table so far away. Obviously, she was not wanted. But at the same time, she was very close to them; she was, she finally realized, the banquet table itself, at which the newlyweds sat. Short legs under the table were continually kicking her; the white netting draped against her sides itched. The tiered wedding cake, the meats, platters of delicacies, candelabra, flowers, silver, were heavy; they bent her back under their burden. She was tired of holding up all this weight! She almost wept with pity for being a banquet table.

Margaret listened: Matthew and Mrs. Leopardi were playing a duet. The violin bows—*blows*, Margaret thought— seemed to saw against her nerves. She considered pouring herself another teeny little sip of pinot noir, then reconsidered; she'd already had more than her daily allotment, and she didn't need a headache in the morning. She drew in her breath. They were playing Mozart, with Matthew striving unsuccessfully to stay on key. Mozart's music was annihilated, as flat and dusty as the composer's bones. Such noble music, for such an ignoble end. And Matthew would never play better, Margaret feared.

"Why do people have children?" she asked herself aloud. An answer presented itself at once: To defeat transience. To wound death. But children's helplessness, their dependence, inevitably constrained their parents' lives. And what were the compensations? Margaret hadn't a clue.

When she heard the lesson end, the front door close, and Mrs. Leopardi leave, Margaret shut her eyes and focused on her breathing. Breath in, breath out. When Matthew burst in at her door, freed at last from the torments of Mozart, cocking and firing his Air Blaster and shattering any remaining peace in the room, she almost cried out.

"Come on," Matthew begged. "Won't you please play one game? One? I promise I won't ask for more."

"Are you going to take your bath?" Margaret asked. "Are you going to go to bed?"

"But it's not time," Matthew protested. "It's only eight o'clock." Then, "Dad's the only one that plays with me."

Margaret found it difficult to be patient, but she tried. "Matt, you play with your friends all day," she said. "Why do you need to play with me, tonight? *Why?*"

"Because," Matthew said. He looked embarrassed, seeing his stepmother's strained face. He grew restive. "Because," he repeated, quite at a loss. Then, finding an answer, he put down his toy gun and held up his hands. Margaret watched as he pointed to himself. Then, slowly but accurately, he spelled out the letters that the man from the school for the deaf had taught. When he finished, he pointed to her. Then he looked at the floor.

Margaret did not answer immediately. She would not have known what to say if she'd tried. Finally she took Matthew's Air Blaster and with deliberation fired it, a great puff of oxygen, at her heart. Then she wrapped Matthew in her arms, holding him so tightly that he squirmed like a cat to get free. "No fair! No fair!" he shouted. She released him, but he did not move away, and she held Matthew's body against hers, his thin shoulder blades jutting like awkward wings against her chest.

"Let's pretend we're between the cliff and the river," he whispered. "There's a gang coming after us with machetes. What do we do?"

It seemed to Margaret that she could feel herself falling, and she knew the cold currents of the river. But she said, "Jump! Jump! And we'll swim for it."

HARVEST YEARS

Calla, Darrell, and Alma Jean finally agreed to get Mrs. Haskins, a day woman, for Grandpa. Calla had been all for an old folks' home, which she called a retirement community, but she was outvoted. "You'll see I was right," she nonetheless insisted, offended the way people who are always right are always offended. "My friend Leroy Atlas did a complete survey at his own expense. And it says right here"—she put her finger on Leroy's note and made us read it—"Harvest Year's Leisure Haven is the best."

"Leroy can't spell worth a crap," I observed.

"Profanity is the sign of a weak mind trying to express itself forcibly," Alma Jean said. Alma Jean is my mother, and every now and then she feels compelled to preach. "Besides," she added, looking closer, "that's not spelling. That's punctuation."

"What?" Calla didn't hear well. "Say again?"

Darrell sighed. He'd voted for a hospice, but insurance regulations limited coverage to six months, after which time the patient must either be recertified or pay all hospital costs. Or die.

"Daddy might live another decade," Alma Jean said.

No one replied to this. Grandpa Roebuck had been amazingly vigorous, it was true. Just last New Year's Day he had drunk a six-pack of beer and watched three football games, hollering "Go! *Go!*" and "Hold 'em!" right along with the other men. He had chewed Red Man since the age of eleven and had no intention of quitting now. Every autumn except for this last one he had bushhogged his back pastures without help, and he repaired his fences and castrated his steers with only one other man. He followed the Farm News avidly and viewed the coming recession as though he were going to live long enough for it to affect him. He had voted the straight Democratic ticket for over seventy years and had never before had an illness bad enough to require a hospital or more than the services of young Doctor Rose, who had administered his checkups at the Medical for the past thirty-four years. Until Grandpa Roebuck had begun spitting bright foamy blood a few weeks earlier, he had acted like a man twenty years younger.

"He might be out of the hospital now," Alma Jean told me, "but he's sitting on a time bomb. If his pulmonary goes, he's finished."

It was true. The doctors had ordered complete bed rest: no farming, no watching razor-edged football games, no arguing, no nothing. He wasn't even supposed to strain in the bathroom; he took a special laxative, Doxidan, to prevent that. And someone had to be with him at all times.

"I can't quit my job to take care of Daddy," Alma Jean said. "Next year I'll be eligible for retirement. If I quit now I'll lose half of it. And I already lost a day's pay for every day I stayed with Daddy in the hospital."

"We all have our own lives to lead," Calla said. She didn't work or have kids at home anymore, but she was still miffed over not getting Grandpa Roebuck into Harvest Years.

So the day woman, Mrs. Haskins, was the answer. She wasn't exactly a nurse—even with Medicare, a registered nurse would eat up Grandpa Roebuck's savings in no time, leaving not a penny for his heirs—but Mrs. Haskins came with the highest recommendations and charged only $15 an hour. She would be with Grandpa all day, from eight until six, six days a week. His children—Calla, Darrell, and Alma Jean—could alternate nights twice a week each. Sundays and Sunday nights were my turn.

Even sitting with Grandpa Roebuck was a trial. He was bothered by jangling telephones, so his phone was almost always turned off. Ditto the television, which he said made him nervous. He did not even want anybody reading at night, as the light from other rooms disturbed his sleep, he said, and it was impossible to close off doors because of the air circulation. So we were all going to bed with the chickens and waking when Grandpa did, at dawn. One Sunday night I heard him rise and go relieve himself in the bathroom for about five minutes. Then he went out on the front porch and sat on the wooden swing. He was just sitting there in his brown pajamas, in the dark, with the mosquitoes having a field day. There wasn't much moon, just a little fingernail sliver that I could see from my window. I could hear the swing creak—it was one of those bench-type swings suspended from the ceiling—and it creaked back and forth, back and forth, while the radium hands on my clock moved from two to three. That and the fan were the only sounds, the swing creaking and the crickets chirring and once in a while an eighteen-wheeler passing on its way to Mobile, over on I-10. I didn't get up because Grandpa Roebuck was still strong enough to get around some by himself, but the next morning when I brought him his eggs and grits I asked him, "What were you looking at last night?" But he just smiled and never said a word. Maybe he didn't hear me.

When I told this to Alma Jean she said, "Don't you let him go out on that porch, he might fall and hurt himself. Bust that artery." With me right there. I've never seen a person die and I don't want to. But what was I supposed to do, tell my own Grandpa Roebuck, who'd taken care of himself and three kids and nine grandchildren (including

Darrell's kids that he and Grandma raised after Darrell's wife died)—am I going to tell this old man who gets around by himself and can still see well enough to shoot the eye out of a rabbit that was raiding his collards just a few years ago—am I going to tell this man that he can't get up and sit at night on his own front porch? I can tell you what he'd tell me if I said that, and it wouldn't be polite. So I just decided that the next time I heard him get up in the dark and go outside I'd get up too and keep him company. But he never did it again.

One of the first things Mrs. Haskins did when she came was to take over breakfast. I can't say that I was too grateful to her or to Grandpa Roebuck for this because I had put in considerable time learning to cook Grandpa Roebuck's eggs exactly the way he liked. That was fried, sunny-side up, in fresh bacon grease. He couldn't have the bacon anymore, doctor's orders, and he wasn't supposed to have eggs either, but that was all he would touch for breakfast and he had to eat something. He wanted the yolk unbroken, whited over a little, not too runny, but not too hard. The albumen had to be firm, holding tight together, the way a fresh egg holds, not running all over the pan like a week-old store egg. The problem was that we had no chickens, as Grandpa quit keeping them when Grandma died; and a store egg is a store egg no matter how you cook it. But what can you do with a man who won't eat anything else for breakfast, except fix what he wants, the way he wants it? So I tried. But the art of the egg eluded me. Damned from the start—any fool knew an egg from a green foam-plastic carton couldn't reach the heights of an egg lifted warm from the nest of an outraged, fluttering hen—my eggs would run, break yolk, spit back, make bays and inlets all over the pan. The grease usually got too hot, so the whites got hard and burned at the edges while the yolk was still raw; or else the grease wasn't hot enough, so that the egg squatted, flat and transparent, staring from its yellow eye. After Grandpa sent back a number of these efforts, I began throwing out the runners-up or eating them myself, using three or four eggs for every one that made it to the breakfast tray. After a while I could produce what I considered very nearly the perfect fried egg: whole, hot, peppered, slippery, fragrant, popping little showers of grease on its way from the pan to the heated plate. I could have had a whole new career as a short-order cook. And although my grandfather wasn't a man given to praise, he did say, twice, that my eggs were almost as good as my grandmother's. So it hurt my feelings when he dumped me and my eggs for Mrs. Haskins and hers, and Mrs. Haskins' not even real eggs, but just the whites. *Poached.*

Right away she had Grandpa Roebuck wrapped around her little claws. From the second week she could do anything she wanted, like the way she rearranged the kitchen.

That kitchen had been arranged by Calla's, Darrell's, and Alma Jean's mother, and for the sixteen years since that lady had died, it had stayed exactly the way she had fixed it, down to the hand-knitted potholders hanging on their brass hooks next to the stove. My grandmother had been a short woman, not much over five feet, so she had all the pots and pans down low, under the counters, the way everybody does. Mrs. Haskins was five foot eight, and she moved the pots to the cabinets on the right of the sink. The dishes that had been in the higher cabinets, sixteen place settings of my grandmother's Blue Willow, she moved down below.

"You think he's going to make dinner for sixteen?" Mrs. Haskins joked when Calla asked her about it. "But he—me for the time being—I use these pots all the time." She laughed, a big horsey laugh that boomed all over the kitchen.

Calla didn't like anybody rearranging her dead mother's kitchen, but she didn't say more about that. When Mrs. Haskins painted the natural wood cabinets, though, she and Alma Jean both spoke their minds.

"The idea!" Alma Jean said when she walked in one night to a kitchen painted yellow. "She didn't say a word to anybody!"

"She sure did," Grandpa Roebuck said. "I like yellow."

"Daddy, you never said one word about wanting anybody to paint this kitchen."

"I didn't know I wanted it until Mrs. Haskins brought it up."

"She's ruined the natural finish."

"She said it was too dirty to get clean." He leaned back on his double pillows and tore off a yellow-brown wad of Red Man. "Guess I ain't been much of a housekeeper."

"Don't these paint fumes bother you?"

"Can't smell no more. Too old, no smeller left. But I see fine, and I like yellow." The way he pronounced *yellow* made it rhyme with *smeller*.

The next afternoon Calla and Alma Jean told Mrs. Haskins privately that any changes in the household must be discussed with them beforehand. After all, Grandpa Roebuck was a very old man, and the house wasn't likely to be lived in too much longer, and there was no point in spending money to fix it up when it was just going to be sold.

"You never know," Mrs. Haskins said. "Your father has always lived an outdoor, active life. He was in remarkable condition, wasn't he, before this current problem? He could live to be a hundred and five. He might as well live in a clean place."

"I've cleaned this place every chance I got," Alma Jean said. Mrs. Haskins could see she was hot over that last remark. "With a full-time job it hasn't been easy."

"I know," Mrs. Haskins said agreeably. She laid her hand on Alma Jean's arm. "You just consider this *my* full-time job now."

That night Alma Jean plugged in Grandpa's phone after he had gone to sleep. "The nerve of that woman," she told Calla. "Can you beat it?"

"*Yellow*," Calla said. "You just can't get good hired help."

Grandpa didn't seem to be getting well, but he wasn't getting worse, either. Mrs. Haskins, an energetic fifty-nine-year-old who kept herself up with Lady Clairol and Mary Kay, seemed to cheer his spirits. She read aloud to him from a magazine she subscribed to called *Inspirational Stories*, which was full of articles by famous people and some not-so-famous, telling how their faith in the Lord had helped them earn another million or get their kids off cocaine or come down off a mountain after their plane had crashed or beat the big C. Grandpa still had eyes like a hawk and could certainly read for himself, but he liked Mrs. Haskins, smelling like White Shoulders, sitting there by his bed. One afternoon when I came in she was finishing a story about a man who was haying his field alone and had driven his tractor up a hillside and then stopped to fix something and the tractor had rolled back down on him, all three tons of it, pinning his legs, but the strength of the Lord had enabled him to dig himself out and call for help. Grandpa was listening to this tractor story like a little kid, not taking his eyes off Mrs. Haskins, who looked very nice with her black hair pulled back tidy and a fresh church-type dress with pearls or what looked like pearls around her neck. It occurred to me, not for the first time, that maybe Grandpa was going a little sweet on Mrs. Haskins, because of the way he perked up around her and had started shaving again, but mostly because he could never resist a religious woman, at least not a good-looking religious woman.

"These are true stories," Mrs. Haskins announced when she finished reading. "They are written by the actual people they happened to. I think when you get well we should send in your story, Mr. Roebuck."

"I don't know what that story would be," Grandpa said.

"You won't know if you won't admit you know." Mrs. Haskins sounded real irritated, not a bit sympathetic.

"The doctors said you'd get better once you got your strength back," I offered. The doctors had said no such thing, but I thought I sounded convincing. "You've got to try," I finished.

"If I can't do nothing," Grandpa said with logic, "I don't reckon there's much call to try."

"I'm not listening to negative thinking," Mrs. Haskins said. She got up and headed for the kitchen.

"I didn't say I wasn't trying," Grandpa added hastily.

"Well, *you'd better.*" Mrs. Haskins didn't say what she was going to do if he didn't try to get well, but she sounded pretty final. She acted like it was a personal insult to her if Grandpa didn't eat what she fixed, or go for a little walk around the house every day, or watch the afternoon Farm

Report on TV. And the odd thing was, he actually stopped losing so much weight and started dressing again in the daytime, as if he were expecting visitors or might go out for a drive.

By midsummer, when I'd come over for a visit he'd be sitting up in his vinyl-covered green recliner. He'd be wearing his plaid shirt and khakis, but as soon as Mrs. Haskins left he'd undress and go to bed.

"An aneurysm is nothing to play mind games with," Calla told me one Sunday evening when she came over to get some frozen pole beans Grandpa had put up from his garden last summer. "She's making Daddy very tired. The doctor made it clear that he's not supposed to strain. Not in any way at all." Her eye fell on the bottle of Doxidan on the kitchen counter. The little amber container was nearly full.

"Has he been taking his laxatives?"

"She's stopped giving them to him."

"She's what?"

"Now that he's eating better it isn't much of a problem."

"Better ask the doctor about that!"

"He seems to be OK."

"That woman's going to kill Daddy!"

The telephone's ring cut us off. Lately it had been plugged back in because Mrs. Haskins had convinced Grandpa that nervousness was all in the mind and it wasn't good for him to cut himself off from the world. Calla answered just as Grandpa hollered, "Hey! Get that!" She brought the phone to his bed and sat on the staircase while he talked. The call was brief, less than two minutes, and when it was over Grandpa laid the receiver into its cradle with elaborate care.

"Who was that?" Calla demanded.

"Pete." Pete was one of the boys Grandpa had raised after Darrell's wife had died.

"What'd he have to say?"

"Just telling me how he was working late a lot. He's been working late a lot."

"He has time to play baseball three times a week," Calla said, "but not time to come see his own sick Grandpa."

"He's coming by Saturday morning," Grandpa said, sinking back on his two pillows.

"That'll be a first," Calla said. "Not one of Darrell's kids has come yet, much less stayed the night or offered to help around this place. And here Faith lives two miles down the road."

"Saturday morning," Grandpa said.

"He must want something."

Grandpa rolled over onto his side. "He wants to borrow my bass boat," he said. "Now unplug that damned phone. The ringing makes me nervous. I hear it in my ears."

Calla got her frozen beans and smiled at me in a confidential way. She was never sorry to be one up on Darrell. Her own kids didn't visit either, but then they lived in another town, twenty miles away.

That was the way it was that summer. Mrs. Haskins came every day, punctual as sunshine and just as optimistic. It wasn't a month before she had cleaned everything in the house and started on the yard. My grandmother had been a big one for flowers and I can remember when I was a kid the yard being full of them, crowded up so thick to the fence that all you saw was color. You could smell them clear inside the house. Most of them were gone now, of course, except for the perennials, which were overgrown with weeds; but Mrs. Haskins started bringing her gardening gloves and in one week she had torn out all the strayed monkey grass and transplanted it back into borders, which gave the daylilies a chance to bloom. Then she bedded zinnias, pansies, salvia, and snapdragons, with gladiolas in the back, almost like my grandmother used to have. Over the months Mrs. Haskins fertilized and watered, and the flowering olive that hadn't flowered for sixteen years bloomed half the summer long, scattering its blossoms whole on the ground as though bridesmaids had left them there.

"It keeps me busy," Mrs. Haskins said, booming out her horsey laugh. "Mr. Roebuck told me the flowers he likes. And I never could stand being idle. It's really a fault with me."

"She's got her hooks in him," Calla told Alma Jean in late August. "She's after his money. There's no fool like an old fool and he's just fool enough to marry her."

"She's done the world for Daddy, and he appreciates her," Alma Jean said, "but he told me one time,"—she pointed to a portrait of her mother hanging on the wall—"'*that's* the only woman I've ever loved.' He's not about to get married. Why, he can hardly get out of bed."

"It's not getting out of bed he's thinking about."

"Oh, foolishness!"

"Wait and see," Calla said.

"There's laws," Darrell said.

"Her, a widow lady with no pension? You think she wouldn't feather her nest if she got the chance? She's thinking this house is going to be *her* house."

"It's illegal," Darrell said.

"Wait and see," Calla said.

Actually, the longer I stayed with Grandpa, the less it seemed like such a boring thing to do. After a couple of months I even offered to stay on other people's nights. I did a little exploring around Grandpa's pastures and woods and it was all very peaceful. I mean I've visited his farm all my life, but before this I'd never been past the back garden, because of the cows. I'm not about to fool around with cows. Alma Jean told me one time, I couldn't have been more than six years old, about some fourth cousin who had been gored to death right in my Grandpa's own side pasture. Up against the barbed wire fence, which the boy couldn't make it past. Nobody could get the bull off the kid, not the dog or my

grandfather or even this black guy Archie who used to help
my grandpa with his steers and who was supposed to be as
strong as a bull himself. This fourth cousin got tossed on
the ground and gored about four hundred times, then the
bull trotted off like he forgot all about it. So I never went
in a cow pasture in my life, not even when it had just old
cud-chewing Polled Herefords in it. But there were no cows
now; Darrell had sold them. The cow paths were still there,
though, and I followed them, crooked, hoof-dented, illogical
trails that wandered through palmetto to the water oaks
in the woods behind the pastures. You know if palmetto
will grow on a piece of land, it's not good for anything else;
but this land did look handsome. A person lives in the city
long enough, he gets to appreciate a vest-pocket park with
a dog-pee bush and two seesaws on it; and this was actual
land that had belonged to my grandfather and to his father's
father. Knowing that it was going to be sold off as soon as
Grandpa died, which couldn't be too long, made me feel
possessive and sad about it, even though basically it's just
a palmetto patch with some big water oaks on it.

The sun lay in bright splotches between the water oaks,
and the woods opened into another meadow you couldn't see
from the house. Green enough to blind you. Dried-out cow
patties here and there still flattened the grass. I followed a
narrow dried-mud trail to a back-pasture barn that Grandpa
had built himself when he was eighty-two. It wasn't such a

great looking barn, just a kind of lean-to, really, but he had said himself that he never built it for looks. Inside, the odor of decayed hay rose in the quiet heat, but the animal smell had faded. A dirt dobber hovered around my ear until I waved my hand at it. "Can't do nothing," Grandpa had said. "Had to get shed of my cows. Had to get shed of my garden. Can't even cook my own breakfast." No wonder he didn't want to try. Now Calla was wanting to get rid of the one person who could bully him into wanting to try. I had felt perfectly fine until I was standing there in that dark cowbarn thinking about that.

When I got back to the house a little after six, I walked into the middle of a real hair puller, almost, between Calla and Mrs. Haskins. Grandpa was lying in his room looking shriveled and yellow, and on the counter between the dining room and the kitchen was this assortment of his pills, Diabinese, Peritrate, Lasix, Lanoxin, and Doxidan. Calla had her arms crossed in front of her chest and was talking in a very loud voice. Mrs. Haskins was calmer and not so loud but she wasn't letting Calla push her around.

"He's got to take his laxative, the doctor said so and you aren't in charge here, Mrs. Haskins," Calla was saying in the kind of voice you'd use with a smart-aleck kid who needs to be put in his place.

"He's been eating fresh figs and they're a natural laxative." Mrs. Haskins sounded as reasonable as a very put-out person can sound.

"He's not supposed to strain and this shouldn't even need to be said."

Mrs. Haskins lowered her voice so Grandpa couldn't hear and said, "You know he's done it on himself more than once when he's taken those pills." She shook her head and smiled but she was pleading with Calla. "He took one of those pills and couldn't get to the toilet fast enough."

"He's not supposed to strain."

"He's not going to strain. But those pills are too strong and it embarrasses your father terribly to go through that." Mrs. Haskins looked toward the figure slumped in the other room. "He's a very dignified man and we just can't do this to him."

"I think what we're going to need is a registered nurse, Mrs. Haskins. My father is a very sick man and at-home care just isn't working out."

You could see from the expression on Mrs. Haskins' face that this really hit her. "I don't mean . . ." she started.

"You've been awfully good to Daddy, but these medical decisions are not up for debate."

"He's been getting better," Mrs. Haskins insisted.

"I've discussed this with Alma Jean and Darrell and they are with me in thinking this. I'm telling you out of courtesy that Daddy's condition needs professional care."

Mrs. Haskins blinked her eyes a couple of times and her mouth opened a little. She took a deep breath but didn't say anything.

"Naturally we'll give you a week's severance," Calla continued. "Starting tonight. And you won't even have to come back again." Calla went over to the table for her purse and got out her checkbook. I thought for a minute that Mrs. Haskins was going to leave while Calla was writing, but she didn't. I wanted to say something to her, but I couldn't think of exactly how to put it. Mrs. Haskins wasn't looking my way anyhow, so I opened the screen door and slipped out and sat on the back steps. Grandpa wasn't my father and I didn't have any say in the matter, but Calla didn't have the right to can Mrs. Haskins like that, on the spot. As far as I knew, she and Darrell and Alma Jean hadn't discussed this situation at all, and Alma Jean for sure was going to be furious. About the time I made up my mind to go back in and tell this to Mrs. Haskins, I heard her going down the driveway in her old Toyota, her tires crunching the shell.

Alma Jean was certainly upset. She was all for calling Mrs. Haskins immediately and asking her to please come back, it was a misunderstanding. "How are we going to find anyone like her?" Alma Jean kept repeating.

"We aren't," Calla said. "I told you we needed to put Daddy in Harvest Years to begin with, and if you all had listened to me, we wouldn't be having this messiness right now."

"I'm not doing it," Alma Jean said. "I'm not putting my own father in an old folks' home. Especially that place. Why, they shuffle those old people from room to room like they're shuffling a pack of cards, and it confuses them. I've smelled urine in their hallways and I've heard that the kitchen staff buys refuse produce. Daddy's lived in this house all his life and he's going to die in it. If he could take care of all of us, the least we three can do is take care of him."

"I've got my own life to lead," Calla said. "I can't sit here every night. If you and Darrell want Daddy at home, you can take care of him yourselves. Let him come live with one of you."

"Harvest Years is very clean," Darrell said. "They've got nurses and a doctor comes in every day."

"I'm working," Alma Jean said, "or I would do it. But I can't quit my job and give up my whole retirement. Just a few more months."

"I've done more than my share already," Calla said.

"Leroy runs a good ship," Darrell said. "You shouldn't believe that gossip. His wife takes personal charge of the staff. And we could get a discount."

For a week and a half Mrs. Haskins visited grandpa, bringing the *Inspirational Stories*. Once when I was there she read about a boy whose mother had fixed a torn button-hole on his shirt, stitching it just right about thirty or forty times, even though the mother was tired and had thought about just letting the buttonhole go since it was only a little boy's shirt. And then the little kid fell out of a tree he was climbing, and wouldn't you know, a branch caught his shirt by the buttonhole? And the buttonhole held him until the kid's hollering brought his mother out to see what was wrong and she took him down. Grandpa enjoyed that story.

But Mrs. Haskins got another job before too long and couldn't come much after that. I got a job working the night shift at Denny's and that wears you out night and day, so I didn't come as much as I wanted, either. Not that I didn't mean to. You can imagine I was pretty bothered when I heard that Grandpa Roebuck had gotten into a big row with his nurse at Harvest Years, not a registered nurse at all but some kind of training nurse who had told him that he couldn't be getting up at night and walking around because he might fall down and endanger himself. I have to side with my grandfather because he didn't get up that much anyway, and he used his walker when he did. So he said he was getting up when he pleased and she said he wasn't, and they got pretty tight about it, and she told Grandpa she was going to have him tied to his bed if he didn't behave. She said she didn't actually tie him, but only threatened to. That was when Grandpa's aneurysm gave way. Alma Jean said that artery went like a tire that had a blowout. Darrell said he was going to sue Harvest Years; but Leroy, who owns the place, is a lawyer and said Grandpa Roebuck died of natural causes which any fool doctor anywhere could testify to. And Grandpa Roebuck being ninety-plus years old, what could you expect? So all Grandpa's grandchildren came to see him at last, Pete and Faith and all of them, and said how glad they were that they didn't have to see him the way he was at the end, so they could remember him the way they wanted; and they sat in the front family pews while the organist played "Beyond the Rainbow" and "The Old Rugged Cross." Brother Gluck read from the twenty-first psalm and said how a good man's life lives after him in his works and in his children's lives. Handkerchiefs were out all over the room and at the end everybody filed past to look at the old man lying on white satin, his yellow spotted hands with the farmer's fingernails thick as horn crossed over his chest, and him looking smaller than I remembered, dressed in a black suit Darrell had bought for the occasion. Calla took off his wedding ring for a keepsake and I took the white Bible that came in the center of the big spray of red roses the family sent. I never saw so many flowers in my life, carnations and spider lilies made into a cross, and loads of mums and gladiolas. The funeral parlor smelled like Grandma's front yard on a summer's day.

They laid him down under a striped canopy, next to my grandmother, with everybody standing on a carpet of artificial grass that covered the dirt. Mrs. Haskins stood in the back and cried her eyes out, and the family stood up front, crying out theirs. The only person who didn't was Alma Jean, who was already cried out, I guess.

SEMENOVA

My earliest education in ballet came from a five-foot-tall, wire-thin woman named Madame Semenova, who rumor had it was a former mistress of Stalin. I met her because my aunt, an opera singer fallen on hard times, was the pianist for Madame's ballet classes in return for minimal compensation and Madame's willingness to teach me, the eight-year-old niece, the fundamentals of dance. Semenova was, in my aunt's words, a tyrant, a bully, but an immensely gifted artist who at the age of twelve had joined the Ballet Russe de Monte Carlo. Later, she was the premiere danseuse with the Paris Opera Ballet. She offered a rare opportunity, my aunt said, not to be missed, and I must take advantage of it.

"It's not remarkable that she was a star," Mama replied, "if she was really Stalin's mistress."

"What is that?" I asked. "What is a mistress?"

Mama ignored me but my aunt's eyes opened wide. "That's a rumor! Don't say anything!"

Mama made no secret of her disdain for my aunt's arty friends, but she withheld out-and-out condemnation with the kind of condescension sisters-in-law sometimes reserve for one another. Besides, as a girl, my mother had always wanted to take ballet lessons herself, so she agreed: she would take me to meet Semenova. If I liked to dance, and if Semenova passed Mama's inspection, then I could learn from her.

My aunt suggested we pick Semenova up on our way to the studio, which would give us all a chance to chat. Moreover, it seemed that whoever drove my aunt also had to drive Semenova. Mama indicated what she thought of ladies who couldn't learn to drive, but she agreed to chauffeur.

Although we had been told to pick Madame up at five, it wasn't until five fifteen that she emerged from her apartment, stone-faced, carrying a thin cane, and wearing a green and purple caftan. Her black hair was pulled into a bun from which one long, loose strand escaped. She got into our car with a bit of difficulty; she was a bit lame. Mama had already informed my aunt, "I'm not calling anybody 'Madame,'" and my aunt was already nervous. Seeing her caught between two forces majeures like my mother and Semenova, I didn't blame her. My aunt and I, in the back seat, exchanged glances. She covertly pretended to be saying a prayer, and that made me laugh. But in fact my aunt hadn't even completed the introductions before Semenova turned to my mother and said, "One thousand six hundred North Boulevard." Her voice, I remember, was the deepest female voice I had ever heard. She pronounced each word very deliberately and slowly, and she had the same trouble with r's as my aunt. I was disappointed that a genuine Russian should sound so French.

"One thousand, six hundred," Semenova repeated. "Hurry. We are late." She exhaled authority.

"You'll have to describe where that is," my mother replied. "I'm not a taxi driver. And if we're late, perhaps you should have been on time?"

In the back seat, my aunt paled. Fourteen seconds and already things were bad.

Semenova, too, was taken aback, and she didn't give my mother any more orders. "Gabrielle," she said, turning with a stiff smile to my aunt, "can you tell us how to find our street? I pay no attention to these things."

My aunt gave directions, and for the duration of the ride, her voice made the only conversation in the car: a solo performance. The rest of us sat in silence. Semenova lifted a silver engraved compact from her purse and put more lipstick on an already enameled mouth. When she turned her cheek I could see a long scar, extending from under the left side of her chin and slanting at an angle past the lobe of her ear. The scar, heavily made up and powdered, was partly hidden by the loose strand of her hair, but when she turned her head I could see the dull violet wound, long healed, against the chalk of her cheek. Nor was the rest of her face beautiful—to me she seemed an old woman—but strong Russian bones underlay her skin, which was still smooth except for the scar. Black liner and mascara heavily encircled her eyes, and she wore silvery dust on her lids. Her mouth was a blood-red slash. She certainly did appear theatrical, although I wouldn't have known that word then. People in our town did not look like Semenova.

Mama concentrated on her driving and ignored us all. My aunt kept up a monologue about what a challenging discipline dance was, how it developed grace and carriage. How it inspired confidence. How all the little girls loved it. I slid deeper into my seat and waited.

Mama dropped us off at the studio and promised to be back in an hour. Inside, the little girls waiting did not appear to love dancing at all. They clustered against the walls and came forward only when ordered to do so by Madame. A rack hung with yellow practice tutus had been rolled into a corner, but everyone wore black leotards and pink tights; Madame allowed no individualities of dress. Shoes were the only status symbol. Those who had danced for three or four years had real toe shoes, with the padded, squared, coveted boxes at the ends. I watched as these older girls laced their shoes with long pink ribbons. To wear such shoes, to be able to stand on one's toes, seemed to me a wonderful thing. I slouched under the barre in my virginal soft slippers, trying to make myself invisible.

"Girls! Girls!" Madame Semenova said. She coughed up the *g*'s like someone clearing her throat and raised her thin cane like a conductor lifting a baton. "On the floor!"

Everyone grouped instantly into military lines in the room's center. Then at a signal the girls sat on the floor, their legs straight out in front of them, their arms at their sides. Fourteen of us were reflected in a mirrored wall, which also doubled the image of a chandelier with some of its crystals missing. A barre and second mirror ran the length of the opposite wall. The panes in the French doors had been painted over to make them opaque. The room was cold, the floor colder. It smelled humid, like stale, prepubescent sweat. I took a place off center in a middle line, surrounded on all sides, I hoped, by allies. But no one spoke to me, and as soon as I whispered, "What do we do?" to the girl ahead of me, I found out why.

"You!" Semenova pinned me with her eyes. My flesh shrank. "Do what the others do, if you can, and be quiet! Music!"

My aunt started playing the piano.

"One," Madame said, raising her cane.

Everyone sitting on the floor spread her legs into a wide V.

"Two," Madame said.

The girls reached forward and each grasped her right foot with her left hand.

"Down."

All heads bobbed obediently toward the right knees.

"And up—"

Fourteen heads went up, one belatedly.

"And back—"

My head refused to come anywhere near my knee.

"And up—"

Up was a tremendous relief.

"And back—"

Madame walked down the line and halted beside me. The music stopped. "Your head is not down," she observed.

"I'm trying," I said. My knees were literally quivering.

"Try harder."

I lowered my head perhaps another half-inch closer to my knee. Madame put her hands on my shoulders and pushed.

"Oh!" It hurt.

"You are young, this is nothing," Madame said. "Left!"

All the heads slid obediently to the left. Yet even with their heads fastened to their knees, I could feel thirteen pairs of other eyes straining out of their corners to see what came next.

Madame Semenova pushed my shoulders down farther. I heard my breath leave my body and felt the back of my knees catch on fire.

Semenova did not let go. But after a while she appeared to grow tired of pressing my head and shoulders down and said, "Everyone up."

Much scrambling about. "You," Semenova said to a red-headed long-haired girl who looked about twelve. Madame appeared to know no one's name. She inclined her head toward me. "Show this one how to bend."

The chosen one flashed a sycophantic smile from which self-assurance nonetheless gleamed. She pranced to a wall, then sat again on the floor, with her spine upright and her back pressed flat against the wall. Madame Semenova raised her cane. The girl planted her right heel firmly against the wall to her right, then her left heel on that part of the wall to her left, making a perfect seated split. Madame lowered her cane. The girl then bent from the waist and lowered her forehead, with apparently no effort, to the wooden floor, while her heels remained against the wall. Her red hair tumbled into a pool on the planks. No one in the class changed expression.

"Without this kind of flexibility," Madame said, "no one can expect to be a dancer."

I looked at my aunt, but she appeared to have retreated into a reverie.

The rest of the session went the same. If I was not ignored or following the other girls as best I could, then I was made the object of a lesson: here is one who knows nothing, show her something. Madame called the names of the steps—in French—but demonstrated little herself; the girls did the work. We stretched against the barre, we took all the positions, we practiced the port de bras, and I was given no quarter for being new, I was expected to follow along and shamed when I could not. Occasionally Madame would walk about the room lifting an arm here or straightening a leg there (and woe to the girl who did not get it right the second time), but mainly Semenova sat on a high stool, supervising and flourishing her thin cane. The lesson was not half over before I had decided that I hated the redheaded girl, I hated my aunt for staging this, but most of all I hated Semenova, who, if a pupil's performance did not meet her expectations, would use her cane to whack the student, hard, on the offending leg. I was later told that on some she raised welts, red swollen stripes.

"Now, turns," Madame said, and the girls lined up, waiting in the corner. What new punishment was this? My aunt resumed her labors at the piano, and the redheaded girl launched herself diagonally into the space across the room, in the direction of the yellow tutus. She extended her arms and, keeping her eyes steadily fastened upon an imaginary spot in the room's far corner, she flew across the floor, turning and turning, looking ahead as long as she could while her body turned, her eyes fixed to keep her body's balance. She spun eight or ten times, rapidly, before finishing lightly on her toes, with that same triumphant, artificial smile.

"Good," Madame Semenova said. "Good!" It was the first time I heard her use that word.

When the second girl was halfway across the room, Madame lowered her cane again, saying, "Now!" and the third girl, then the fourth, swung out without a moment's hesitation. I was at the line's end, hoping to get some visual practice before making my debut. This didn't look impossible. My cousins and I often played at twirling in the back yard, spinning across the grass until we dropped. This might be something I could do. Now and then Madame would interject, "Keep a straight line!" or "Quickly now!" I was determined to do well, tired of being the goat. I would never, I knew, come here again, I never wanted to see Semenova again, but I passionately wanted to perform those turns to perfection. My heart beat faster as the line shortened. The ends of my fingers tingled, full of a life of their own. I silently rehearsed Madame's rules: The carriage of the arms must be open, wide, and out; the elbows flexed, the fingers loose and graceful; the line must be long and the neck proud. Always step ahead, never to the side. Above all, do not lose sight of that imaginary dot in the far corner of the room. Keep your eyes on it until your head must turn or its stem will snap. That will save you. I rehearsed these things as my body waited.

"Now!" Madame said, and I stepped, toe out, into the room. The music kept a heavy, almost palpable beat; I could feel my aunt willing me on. I made a little rhyme in my head:

> One and turn and
> two and turn and
> don't lose sight of
> where you're going
> or you'll fall down . . .

Rhythm, body, mind, all became one focus upon that imaginary dot in the corner of the room. All went well at first but when I passed the center of the room I began to feel dizzy, drunk the way we became when I played with my cousins at home. Still I would not slow down, I had to prove what I could do. I focused upon that spot, I kept my head steady, keeping my eyes on that endpoint as well as I could. Another turn, then another, then the next to last, and I could feel myself wobbling. The corner I had aimed for seemed nowhere near. I was off center, and then I hit something. Did I hear someone titter? The room was spinning! I staggered, recovered, staggered again, and fell into a heap of yellow tutus. I had knocked over the rack.

My pride was hurt more than anything else, but I had to struggle to keep the tears from coming. The girls stopped giggling and Madame stood over me, her red mouth severe. "Get up," she said.

"I won't," I replied, terrified at the words that had flung themselves out of my mouth. That it was my mouth surprised me as much as the words. I was sure Madame was going to beat me with her cane. I closed my eyes and waited. Surely my mother would return and there would be certain vengeance, but that was not now. I stayed on the floor.

"Get up!" Madame said again.

I hid my face under my wing and waited for the blows.

"The child is afraid to move," I heard my aunt say.

Madame jerked me off the floor with a grip like one of Stalin's secret police. She shook me upright the way someone grabs a cat that is about to be thrown out. Then when I was standing up, she shook me twice more to make sure I was on my feet, and she tilted my head sharply back so that I was forced to look at her.

"American children," she said. Her voice was full of contempt.

"My mother says you aren't a dancer!" My words burst out. "You were only a star because you were a *mistress*. You haven't danced at all!"

Madame's scar went white.

"Oh no, no no no!" my aunt said. "Tatiana, she doesn't know what she's saying!"

Semenova's eyes were as unreadable as black ice. Her scarlet mouth stretched into a mask. At the time I believed she was capable of murdering me on the spot, and that only my mother's imminent return would prevent it. There was a long, terrible silence during which I hardly dared breathe. Then she lifted her chin, with its ruinous violet line, and unpinned her hair as though she were caressing it, letting it fall about her shoulders. When she spoke it was as if to herself. "A beautiful woman, a powerful man . . . People talk. There will always be envy! But only an artist creates art.

"When I was sixteen years old," she continued, "I had been a dancer longer than you have lived. I knew what it was to work eight hours, nine hours, then two hours more, sometimes not stopping even to eat. I practiced the same movement hundreds, thousands of times for an audience of only the mirror, so that when the moment came—one moment!—I could abandon my will to the soul of the music. The body does not lie. But neither will it yield its truth to an undisciplined spirit."

She looked at me a long time before going on.

"One night during the war, I was dancing on a stage damaged by bombs, and my leg went through a weak board. It severed the cartilage of my knee, it double-fractured my arm. I would never dance professionally again."

With this she stepped in her stocking feet into the room's center. "But I will always be a dancer," she said, her eyes still locked on mine. As she began to move across the floor, to no sound other than her own footfalls, slowly and yet more slowly, I watched her scarred face transform itself; she was lifted by a music that was audible only to her. Semenova moved carefully, but every movement was in harmony with every part of her body; in the line of her back, the extension of her neck, in the intensity of her expression, she evoked an ephemeral enchantment, the magic of bones and flesh. Never, though I have watched ballet for the rest of my life, was I ever to see again a stage more transformed than this bleak, cold, too brightly lit room.

When she finished, I realized my mother was standing near the door. How long she had been there, I couldn't say, so intent had I been upon the dancer. Mama held out her arms for me as I ran to her. "Your child will be too tall," Semenova said. "She is already almost as tall as I. She can never be a dancer. I would be wasting my time."

My aunt tried to object, but my mother silenced her with a look.

"No one here wants to waste time." Mama turned to Semenova. "Is your class over now? Because we are ready to go and we are not going to wait." Mama gripped my hand and asked me, "Are you ready to go?"

I looked for the last time at the long mirrors reflecting the cold room, at the barre that ran its length, at the huddled girls and the yellow tutus spilled into a froth in the corner.

I did not say a word. Semenova's dancing had transported me into another world, beyond the painted windows of those battered French doors into a realm of silver dust, of a swirling violet-and-green caftan, of a beauty that is fundamental. For the first time in my life, I had seen music visible and heard what could not be said with words.

"Are you ready to go?" my mother asked again. In those days she was sometimes an impatient soul.

No, I was not ready. No, I never wanted to leave.

MATTHEW, NINETEEN

"*I*'m waiting for my cousin," Matthew says, standing with his phone in his hand at his dorm room's window, studying the rain. "Ed's meeting me at noon for brunch. He needs to leave in a couple hours, so he won't be staying long."

"Call me as soon as he's gone," Kirby says. "I've been studying all morning, and I need a break. I could use brunch, too."

It's a broad hint, but he's not going to take it. He hasn't seen his favorite cousin in weeks, not since Ed drove up from New York, helped him move into the upperclassman dorm, treated him to Chinese food, and returned to New York, all in the same day. Plus there is something Matt needs to talk about with Ed. Privately.

"I'll see you this afternoon," he says to Kirby. "After five o'clock?"

"We need to finish our lab report. How are we going to do that if we don't start until five?"

His chemistry partner sounds annoyed; Matthew thinks she sounds like somebody's nanny. He can't imagine how one of his best friends ever fell in love with her. Kirby does a lot for people, but she also makes demands. If you do what she wants, she can be kissy-sweet; but if you don't, she can turn stone cold. He also doesn't like the way she treated his friend.

"Hey," he says, "I think I see Ed now."

Which is not a lie. Coming up the walk between two rows of maples in front of Matt's dormitory, his cousin is hurrying, dodging the rain.

"You need an umbrella!" Matthew yells from his third-floor window. Ed looks up and waves, getting wetter. Then Matt says to Kirby, "It's him, all right."

"Call me as soon as he leaves, Matt," Kirby repeats. "I don't want this report hanging over my head all day."

"I have to go," he says. "He's here."

"I like it, dude, I like it," Ed says, inspecting Matthew's room. Ed has been on a mini-vacation with his girlfriend. After two days of leaf peeping on the Mohawk Trail, the girlfriend has left to visit her parents and Ed is stopping to see Matt, with presents: a sheepskin rug for the new dorm room; a

Vermont cheese from the birthplace of Calvin Coolidge; a red plaid shirt; and, very cool!—a vinyl album containing Matthew's favorite Beatles song, "Tomorrow Never Knows."

Matt spreads the sheepskin on his futon, thanks his cousin profusely, and puts on the record. With Ed there, the dorm feels almost like home.

"Where're your roommates?" Ed asks cheerfully.

"They went camping," Matthew says. "They invited me, but I kind of like the privacy. Like this is the first time everybody's been gone at once."

"Sounds like you need a little down time."

"Yeah, a little think time."

"Always thinking." Ed laughs, and Matt does, too.

On their way to the dining hall, Ed wants to know about girls. Matthew shepherds him past bacon, eggs, and bean-stuffed pita bread. Under the gaze of dead college masters lined in portraits on the walls, he stakes out one of the scarred, heavy oak tables.

"The problem," Matthew says, impaling a piece of waffle with his fork, "is that every single girl here is going with somebody. There is not one exception." He has met plenty of girls and they are mostly friendly, but in their rooms they have photos of their boyfriends propped next to their computers. He'd heard about a girl in another dorm who'd ordered a plastic-coated banner with her boyfriend's name on it, then she'd cut the banner in the shape of a four-foot phallus. Matthew wonders what it would feel like to be the object of such attention. If he did that with a girl's name on a cutout of boobs, he'd be crucified. Of course, he knows girls; he dated a few in high school who made it clear they liked him: Tracy Johnston, who had been in the school play with him; and Amy, not a bad sort and even good-looking in a female jock-ish kind of way, but who was taller than he was and got pimples on her chin every time she got her period. On his seventeenth birthday, Amy had given him a rose. But that was nothing compared to a photo next to a girl's computer or a four-foot banner. "I would just like some kind of real relationship," he tells Ed.

"That doesn't seem impossible," Ed says.

"Actually, it is."

He continues, because Ed might find this mildly interesting but no one else he knows would, "There was this one girl at the campus post office yesterday morning—she was pretty cute except she had an S shaved on the back of her head—she was getting her mail at the same time I was getting mine. And she happened to say, 'My cousin is coming tomorrow and here's a letter from him.' And I said, 'Hey, *my* cousin is coming tomorrow. Are you sure we aren't related?' And she goes, 'What's your name?' So I tell her, 'Matthew Christian Rowlander.' 'Rowlander?' she says. '*Christian*? No, I don't think so. I'm Jewish.'"

"Maybe she wanted you to ask *her* name," Ed suggests.

"No, it was a brush-off," Matt says. "I mean, her tone. I've never been put down for my religion before."

"Maybe she has, and she just wanted you to know she was Jewish."

"Why should I care if she's Jewish?"

"Well, she cares, obviously."

"Which is exactly what I'm talking about. She doesn't want to get involved with anybody but Jewish guys."

"Maybe. But maybe you're overthinking it."

Matthew lapses into silence, sorry he brought it up. What is obvious is that his cousin, his cool, medical-school, athletic, good-looking cousin, has no idea of what it feels like to be brushed off.

"Just wait a few weeks," Ed advises. "These girls will be changing their minds. Their boyfriends may be a thousand miles away. You're here, Matt."

Matthew, whose mouth is full of waffle, makes a sound intended to convey polite but firm disagreement. He swallows and says, "You remember Rich? My friend who went with Kirby the dancer? They broke up."

"I remember them both."

"Kirby told Rich last month that they should both see other people."

"Exactly what I'm talking about."

"She's meeting a ton of people this year and Rich isn't, because he likes to come here on the weekends. She thinks if she weren't available, he'd meet people where he is. So she's told him not to come, and she's met about a hundred guys."

"You think that's a function of her more outgoing personality?"

"I think it's a function of her ginormous breasts."

Ed laughs. Kirby does have large breasts.

"She ditched him." Matt makes a motion like someone flicking away a gnat. "Just like that. She claims he never says anything interesting."

Although he doesn't remind Ed of it—because Ed already knows—Matt remembers a big party at his old classmate Alexa's house, right before high school graduation, when Alexa's parents had been away. The house was palatial: it opened, in back, upon three acres of lawn. Trees thickened as the property rolled down to a bayou which wound along a ravine several hundred yards distant. The warm summer day had faded, slowly, into an equally warm summer dusk. Beside the bayou fireflies had come out, a sight rarely seen in the city. But here at Alexa's house in the suburbs, all was bucolic as a midsummer night's dream. Someone suggested a swim in the pool, although nobody had brought a suit. In their underwear the friends greased a watermelon and played take-away in the water. Everybody was drinking IPAs, which didn't really agree with Matthew, who had never liked beer. But that evening he drank three. Then someone—who?—thought it would be fun, in the dark, for everybody to take off their underwear and hide. You had to keep your eyes strictly to yourself for fifteen seconds while each person streaked to a hiding place. The house was off limits, so nearly everybody fanned to the woods. If you were seen coming back, whoever saw you got a point on you. Whoever gave up the least points, won.

Matthew kept on his shorts, as did most of the others. He decided not to go for the woods—the obvious choice— because, even though the trees and shrubs offered excellent cover, their distance from the house made the likelihood of one's being seen fairly great. So he'd hidden in the gardener's tool shed on the theory that a tool shed wasn't the house, and was therefore fair game. He'd been fast and had rushed out, as if to the woods—he made sure everyone could hear him go—but then he'd circled, with speed and stealth, back around to the shed. Opening its heavy door, he'd lowered himself noiselessly behind a wheelbarrow that was parked in front of a broken ping-pong table now used to support paint cans and roller brushes frozen in trays of old latex. He'd been squatting behind the wheelbarrow, half under the ping-pong table, congratulating himself in advance on having won, when, soundlessly, Kirby entered the shed.

And at once he could see what Rich sometimes talked about. Although Matthew had known Kirby for years—and had seen her in various stages of undress, from dance programs at school in which she wore the same tights and leotards as the other girls, to this swim party in her bra and underpants—he realized now that he had never seen her at all. People kidded (except around Kirby, who was understandably sensitive on the subject) about her breasts being so big, but there they *were*, not in a leotard or swimsuit but in wet white lace, practically naked, and five feet away from him. Matthew had felt struck as if by lightning, electrified. He had an instant and painful erection, then became acutely aware of his embarrassment and shifted, slightly, to better hide himself. Kirby turned, startled; Matthew simultaneously whispered, "One point, Kirby!"

She bit her lip and grew red-faced, then laughed softly. "Shut up," she threw back, "or everybody'll have a point." And she hid on the far side of the gardener's riding lawn mower.

They had been correct in their surmises, independently made, that a hiding place close to home base, as opposed to being in the trees, would afford them ultimate victory; and, as Matthew had one point fewer than Kirby, he won. Kirby came in second. Rich, who'd exhaled all his breath and sunk himself to the bottom of Alexa's parents' pool, had been seen by somebody virtually every time he surfaced, and he came in last. "Dumb stunt," was Kirby's verdict; Matt called it a brilliant attempt. As far as Matt was concerned, Rich was always the coolest guy in the room. He could do a backflip off a ten-meter board; he had been the first to stand and applaud when Matt was named valedictorian; and he had come up with the idea of the cruise.

At the end of the summer after graduation, Matt, Rich, and four other boys had left for a cruise. It had been Rich's idea, at some point in their senior year, that they all ask for the same graduation gift from parents and grandparents: a cruise from Galveston to Fort Lauderdale. The pack would be together one last time for a trip they'd remember all their lives. After he became the male half of The Kritch—Kirby and Rich—Rich had wanted to change the rules and allow girls on the trip, but he'd been shouted down. There had been high school girls on the cruise with their families, expecting to be bored, who had become ecstatic at the sight of six college freshmen-to-be. All the boys claimed to have gotten laid at least once (except Rich, who was being faithful) and Matthew (who never had any luck); and perhaps Charles had actually succeeded. The week after that, the summer was over. Everybody went off to their separate colleges or universities, Matthew to the Ivy League, Rich to a good state school, the others for points west and south. Only one of his classmates would be attending Matthew's school: Kirby. He couldn't believe the Fates. Amy, who was a first-rate scholar, was going to an obscure women's college in Florida; and here was Kirby, whom he had assumed was never interested in anything but dancing, in the cradle of the eastern schools. That had been just fourteen months ago, and it seemed like fourteen years.

The midsummer night at Alexa's house seemed as remote as a dream. The nights now came on quickly. In October Matthew delighted in watching the maples in his quadrangle change color, but the pragmatist in him knew what January must be. He liked his roommates, but they still weren't tight like his old friends from home, who knew what he thought before he thought it. He participated in intramural soccer, coed touch football, and band; but none of these offered what he was looking for. He had been humiliated at a touch football game when one of the seniors yelled, after Matthew fumbled the ball, "Come on, Rowlander, get in the game!" Matthew had felt real appreciation when Kirby yelled back at the guy, on Matthew's behalf, "And you get a life!"

"So," Ed said, stealing a piece of Matthew's bacon, "How's Rich taking it? Being ditched, I mean."

"Hard. But he's trying to be cool. I mean, he says he thinks it won't break them up. He's going to give Kirby a lot of room . . . not that there's much else he can do. She's not letting him come over here at all. She told me. We went to dinner the other night and she spilled her guts. She definitely wants to meet other guys."

"You took her out?"

"Not on a date," Matthew says. "Rich is my friend."

He frowns, remembering very clearly the wheelbarrow, the ping-pong table, the riding lawnmower, and Kirby in the near-dark of the tool shed, opening the silent door, stepping through a crack of light. The silhouetted outline of her body.

The talk turns to sports, to the dick senior's remark at coed touch football, to the forty-yard touchdown run Ed made five years ago that was actually written up in the Ivy Daily Reporter. Matthew has never been written up for any athletic feat; he has accepted that he is not destined for athletic greatness or even athletic mediocrity.

Then Ed notices a particular college master's portrait, newly arrived on the wall. "I hated his guts," Matthew's mild older cousin admits with surprising heat. "He always favored the English majors. He was obvious about it. If you were in science, if you cared about evidence-based facts, you could forget it, he made you feel second-class." Ed lifts his coffee cup in the direction of the dead master. "He thought a microtome was a tiny little book!" Both cousins laugh, and Matthew feels a sudden pang: *I miss my people so much!* The university was so big, so intense, so far from home!

Ed needs to get on the road and makes Matt promise to spend Thanksgiving with him and his girlfriend in Boston. The stop-and-go rain has given up for the moment and the day's waning sunlight, falling upon the two cousins' faces, makes them look almost beatifically happy. Ed wraps an arm around Matt's shoulder and tells him he'll see him soon. Matthew uses the L-word, the word he is sure he will never be able to use with a girl. Everybody loves everybody in this family. He expresses gratitude again for the red plaid shirt, the cheese from Calvin Coolidge's farm, the record, the sheepskin rug. As it is Sunday afternoon, the traffic in Steeple Street is minimal. When Ed pulls away from the curb, Matthew takes a white Kleenex from his pocket and waves it like a handkerchief. He can feel Ed's grin even though the car is headed away from him. The Honda's window rolls down and Ed waves back. Then Matt is alone again.

He walks back to the dorm, avoiding puddles and the tourists that are present even on this rainy day, and thinks that perhaps he will call Kirby after all, or perhaps he won't. Having her as his lab partner had seemed a good idea when assignments were given out, but now he thinks he would have done better to have made a new friend, teamed up with one of the guys. Or another girl. Or a *woman*, he corrects himself. But the fact is, he does not think of nineteen-year-old girls as women except as intellectual/political abstractions. The females he knows and likes are girls. He does not usually think of himself as a man; but then, he corrects himself again, perhaps he should. Although sometimes he'd just like to retreat; sometimes one gets tired of being correct. If he knew a twenty-one-year-old female, she would be a woman. Matthew, a sophomore, wishes he knew more girls.

The thought of lab work depresses him. It is part of the new life: the soggy weather, the early-fading light, the knowledge that here you are nobody special, just another 1600 SAT score. High school genius turned invisible nerd. He climbs the forty-two stone steps to the third floor and is surprised to find Kirby in his room.

"Your neighbor said you'd be right back," she explains. "It's OK? Your cousin's gone?"

Matthew brightens at the sight of her. He points out the sheepskin on his futon and says, "He brought me this. And a cheese. Want some cheese?"

"No thanks."

"From the birthplace of our thirtieth president."

Kirby laughs and rubs her hand over the sheepskin, inspecting it, then stretches out on it. "Nice," she says. "Very comfortable." She sounds the way Matthew wishes the girl in the mailroom had sounded.

"He brought me a record, too," Matthew says, and puts on the Beatles disc: *float . . . relax . . .*

"Look, it's raining again," Kirby says.

He watches a little knot of tourists disperse. He is not sure he will ever get used to living in a place where there are tourists around all the time. "What lousy weather."

"We could stay here," she says. "We don't have to go to the lab."

"At least it's dry here."

He sits in the room's beanbag chair and takes off his shoes and rubs his feet on the sheepskin; his left foot accidentally touches hers. Matthew draws it back like their toes had kissed. He feels suddenly and totally awkward.

The rain thrums on the roof, sealing the room with humidity. The place now feels too warm; he is warm, but not at all relaxed. Kirby turns on her side, propping herself on her elbow, her breasts falling into the thin cotton of her blouse. She smells good, something he has never noticed before.

She turns her face up and looks at him with a smile, a smile Matthew has seen her give Rich many times. Surely, Matthew thinks, she must know how beautiful she looks. She is a dancer, made for a stage. Does she know what she's doing to him?

He has not finished thinking this when she asks, "Are you tired? You look tired. Listen, let's forget the lab report today. We can go early tomorrow." And she takes his hand and tugs him forward, downward, toward herself. He kneels beside the futon with an almost-overwhelming desire to kiss her, then stops.

"Is this all right?" he asks.

"It's all right," she says.

"With you, with Rich, I mean."

She touches his lips with one finger, then softly, softly, she covers his mouth with her own.

It wasn't as if, in the end, anybody believed that high school romances really lasted. People made promises to each other, and everybody except them knew that the promises would be broken. Even his parents had made promises, and surely they had loved each other; but his mother had grown restless and unhappy, and now his father was happy with someone else. And it wasn't as if Kirby hadn't had the decency to tell Rich. She wasn't just messing around. Rich knew what Kirby wanted. He just didn't know, any more than Matt had known, *who*; and by the time Rich found out, maybe he wouldn't care. Though that was hard to believe, that was a total cop-out, if you thought about it; and Matthew knew he would have to think about it. This evening would not end well, it could not end well. But the evening was not ending, it had hardly begun; and soon he was not thinking, not thinking at all.

CHEATS

$\mathcal{M}$rs. Rowlander, on vacation with her husband, had been in Washington for four days before she finally visited The Wall. She chose a summer day when young people were playing softball on the grass, but the sight of the players did not make Mrs. Rowlander happy. A veteran in his mid-forties, who looked to be about Mrs. Rowlander's age, sat in a wheelchair also watching the players. A sign that he held in his lap announced that he was a victim of Agent Orange defoliant. The sign, scrawled with a Magic Marker and difficult to read, announced that he was dying of cancer. His face and body were more eloquent. Mrs. Rowlander looked away.

"Lots of people have had cancer," her husband said. He had had it himself. "They don't display themselves for pity."

Mrs. Rowlander didn't reply. She and her husband had walked from the Lincoln Memorial, stopping at the Statue of the Three Servicemen. In the distance they could see the black polished granite wall. Although she had never seen it before, Mrs. Rowlander knew what to expect: a memorial that descended into the earth like a grave, incised with the names of all the Vietnam War missing and dead. But she had not expected that the names would be arranged as they were.

"They're not alphabetized," she said, opening her hands in bewilderment at the seemingly endless lists of names of the fallen, arranged chronologically by the date on which they were wounded or died. Because of the cancer-stricken vet, neither she nor her husband had noticed the directories of names near the entrance. "How would you ever find anybody?"

"Are you looking for somebody specific?"

"Actually, I am," she admitted.

"An old boyfriend?"

Mrs. Rowlander smiled. After all these years, Mr. Rowlander could still sound jealous.

"No," she said. "I was looking for a former student."

Her husband lifted an eyebrow.

"I wouldn't even remember his name, except he was connected to my family, sort of . . ."

Mr. Rowlander was listening.

"His name was Grady Edwards," she went on. "He was eighteen years old when I was twenty-four. His father and my mother were friends when they were young, and his father once asked my mother to marry him. His father was the principal of a school."

The account had ceased to interest Mr. Rowlander. His voice briskly returned Mrs. Rowlander to the present.

"This boy died in Vietnam?"

"I don't know," Mrs. Rowlander said.

"You don't know? Then why are you looking for him?"

"He was my student," she repeated. "Our parents almost married each other." She felt helpless to explain any further, except to add, "He could have been my brother."

Mr. Rowlander nodded. War monuments didn't interest him, but he usually went along with what his wife wanted, and she had wanted to visit this place. Now she was reading the names on the wall, starting with the first one. Her progress was slow. Here and there, all along the wall, people had left mementos: flowers in a Coke bottle, or a plastic wreath, or notes; she read those, too. A granite walkway descended gradually, the wall correspondingly grew taller, the lists of names lengthened.

"Let me go check around," Mr. Rowlander said. "There's got to be a directory somewhere. This could take all day."

"No," Mrs. Rowlander said. "I'd rather just look."

"Why?"

"I don't know why," she said. Then, "I'll tell you . . ."

In 1967 she had been Margaret Davis, "Mollie" to her friends, working on a master's degree, paying her way with a teaching fellowship. She taught one class, then two, of Bonehead English, formally known as Remedial Composition, Daily Themes. At the time, the university—better known for its football team than for its academics—functioned under an antiquated state law that required it to admit every graduate of a state high school for at least one semester. The result was that every September three thousand eighteen-year-olds poured onto a campus that could accept only one thousand.

"Look to your left and look to your right," incoming freshmen were told. "Only one of you is going to be here in January." The teaching assistants were instructed, "You must act as the admissions committee. If the students can't do the work, flunk 'em out. First time around." The TAs were armed with a set of grading standards and told to give Fs, without exception, to any student who didn't meet them. The university's survival depended on it, they were told.

It was the first college class Mollie Davis had ever taught, and her pupils were only a little younger than she. For the most part, Mollie liked them: she felt almost one of them herself. Southern-bred, blue-collar, savagely noble and virginally ignorant, they all seemed happy to be away from home, which for the most part was in towns with names like Canton, Denham Springs, Opelousas, Dime Box, Milledgeville, Alexandria, Chinquapin.

And there was Grady Edwards. Mollie looked at him and tried to imagine what her mother might have seen in his father. Young Grady was tall, well over six feet, and skinny: he weighed maybe 145 pounds in his boots. He had the lashless blue eyes indigenous to the Anglo-Saxon corridor that slices through Louisiana-Mississippi-Alabama, and limp brown hair that hung, like everybody else's in the sixties, just below his collar but not rebelliously long. He had the flush of the born redneck, that tender English skin that burns and peels and then burns again before it tans: Grady's face, a face born to anonymity, looked boiled. Except for his height, no one would ever notice him in a crowd. He looked like somebody's kid brother, the kind who borrows your bicycle and then accidentally smashes its fender so that you have to beat him up. Only yesterday he could have been twelve years old. He wore jeans and a plaid shirt like everybody else. Mollie could imagine why her mother had preferred to marry Mollie's own father.

"Grady Edwards!" she had said to him accusingly, that first day she spied his name on her class roll. "Are you from Denham Springs?"

Grady Edwards looked alarmed. He was slouching in the back row with his spine at a 135-degree angle and his legs sticking into the aisle. At the sound of his name he drew up his legs. "Yes ma'am," he said. He looked intimidated, but he managed to ask, "Why?"

"Your father's principal of the high school?"

Oh, *that*, Grady Edwards' face said. "Yes ma'am."

"Thought so." Mollie smiled. She had a pretty smile which even then she used too infrequently. Grady took the smile as a good sign and restretched his legs. Mollie did not call on him again for the duration of the semester. With over twenty students in her class, each of them writing a theme every day, descriptive expository narrative comparison-and-contrast personal, she didn't have time to draw anyone out. She did, however, get to know them from their themes.

Grady Edwards' themes were disasters.

"This is not the Harvard of the South," Mollie said to the graduate assistant with whom she shared a shower-stall-sized office. "Look at this!" She shoved across the desks a scrawled piece of paper ripped ragged-edged from a spiral notebook: "The perduction of suger-cane requires field to be bernt whitch make allot of smoke and fowl air not invionmental but a help, to farmers, with more tonnes." She struck her forehead. "There's a thought in there, there are two or three thoughts, but Sally, I've read the equivalent of three times *War and Peace* in this kind of prose. I think it's destroyed my brain."

Her companion, who was from Minneapolis, found the southern heat more oppressive than the prose. The university had recently installed air conditioning, but the administration had not found it necessary to install it in the graduate assistants' offices. "My brain's just fried,"

Sally said. "Wake me when we get to the Starlight. Order me a Jax."

"I think I'm flunking more than my sixty-six percent," Mollie said. She sighed. "This is terrifically depressing. Maybe I'm not cut out for teaching. I mean, I'm just not getting through. I don't know how I can explain it any more clearly, subjects, verbs, one in each sentence, every goddamn day, and every goddamn day—"

"You need a break," Sally said. "You want to go to the Starlight? You want to get a couple of beers?"

"I majored in English because I wanted to write like Yeats," Mollie said. "Where did I go wrong?"

"I've got three dollars here in change," Sally said, counting out quarters on her desk. "That's plenty for both of us."

Occasionally a batch of themes would be so bad as to keep Mollie awake at night, worrying about the future of her flunkees. Those themes were guilt-inducing. "How can they *be there* with sound waves hitting their eardrums and still keep making the same mistakes? Am I boring them insensible? Should I assign two themes a day?" Mollie announced more frequent office hours and invited them, although without great enthusiasm, to come in and discuss their papers. Nobody came. By November it was clear that at least seventy percent would be returning after Christmas to Canton, Denham Springs, Opelousas, Dime Box, Milledgeville, Alexandria, and Chinquapin. Perhaps,

Mollie told herself, they would get into a junior college or a smaller state school next fall. They surely wouldn't be returning to the Great University.

Final exams approached. Dead Week. Mollie had her own academic work to keep up, and so was only mildly annoyed to learn that the final examination for her course would be a standardized essay, one whose topic would be determined by the department and not left to the individual teacher. "Announce the subject one week prior to the exam so that your students can prepare their thoughts," the department chair said. "But don't let them write their papers in advance. Some will try to cheat. Your job is to see that they don't. All books must be left at the door. Allow them to bring in two sharpened pencils. You'll pass out blue books. Act as your own proctor."

Mollie knew something about cheating, having practiced it on one vividly recalled occasion. She had been in the eighth grade when her teacher announced that he expected his pupils to memorize the Bill of Rights, the first ten amendments, in their given order. Mollie studied them not at all until the night before the test, relying on a good memory to skate her through. But her memory proved more fallible than the amendments. They kept falling out of order. Which came first, Press or Petition? Was Jury Trial sixth, or seventh? She had an inspiration: to write out the Bill of Rights in superfine script and glue them (in order) on the inner frames of her eyeglasses. By removing her glasses and thoughtfully chewing first one earpiece and then the other, she could assure herself of total recall. No matter that in the time it took to prepare this ignominy, she mostly learned the material; she stifled her conscience and prepared to cheat.

But during the test itself, Mollie's teacher had grown suspicious. Mollie's glasses were sitting, semi-folded, on top of her desk when her teacher walked over. Mollie felt tension stiffening her back; she tasted the cotton in her mouth. Her blood hammered in her ears and accelerated her heart. If her teacher had sharp eyes, he could surely see the damning evidence. But what had he seen? He hovered beside her desk, his eyes unwavering upon Mollie. Why he didn't simply seize her glasses and end her misery at once, she didn't know. She thought he might be playing with her, pitilessly, while she sank and sank under her dishonesty. *Panicked ashamed guilty,* her blood said; *stupid ignorant guilty, disgraced guilty.*

And yet she was desperate to deceive more, to get away with her crime, to elude justice. The criminal prayed: O Lord of Junior High Schoolers, please deliver me from Mr. Civics, and Lord, I promise, I'll never never cheat again . . . *Please.* O Lord, you've had mercy on murderers and thieves, why not on me? Let this teacher turn his back for *one second.* Do it, Lord. *Now,* please.

And lo, it happened. Someone down front had a question: a hand rose in the air. The teacher went to answer it. He may have wished for, but did not have, eyes in the back of his head, and Mollie was quick: she did not let opportunity pass. She instantly put her glasses back on; the strips of superfine script were now hidden; she was saved. And for decades afterwards, she could recite the Bill of Rights (although, perhaps, not in order).

Grady Edwards was not so fortunate. Perhaps Grady was too decent to petition the Almighty with such dubious requests; or perhaps his luck simply ran out. In any event, no one distracted Grady's teacher from her vigil. Mollie was an observant young woman, and here was someone cheating: cheating in *her* class. She waited until she was sure of what she was seeing, then she idled to the back row, where Grady crouched, suddenly very intent over his essay. She loomed over the miscreant (her own heart beating possibly as fast as his own) and, granting only enough mercy not to let the rest of the class see what she was doing, she removed, from beneath Grady's trembling hand and his covering essay, the work he had hoped to supply in its place. "See me after class," she whispered. Then she took both blue books back to her desk. Grady Edwards sat there, pink-boiled in defeat. Tears brimmed at his lashless eyes. Mollie avoided looking at him now. She wished he hadn't done it. She wondered what she was going to say.

"Miss Davis," Grady began when they were alone in the room (which took forever to empty of its furiously-scribbling students), "the reason I done it—"

"The reason you *did* it," she interrupted severely, "is that it was the only way you thought you could pass. You have straight Ds and Fs—"

"*No,*" Grady cried passionately. "It's not just the Ds and Fs." His face became very pink and he spoke all in a rush, like a man who is given thirty seconds before the firing squad aims. "Miss Davis, if I flunk out—and if I flunk this course I *do* flunk out—Miss Davis, I'll have to go to Vietnam!"

Mollie paused; she drew in a breath and looked down. Of course he was right, although the thought hadn't occurred to her. It was 1967, the war had escalated under LBJ, and young men who flunked out of college were drafted at once. If Mollie had ever seen cannon fodder, it was standing before her now.

"If I could stay at the university one more semester," Grady pleaded, "I know I'd make it. I'd study more, I haven't done good—"

"You haven't done *well,*" Mollie said fiercely.

"I know," Grady abjectly agreed. "I know."

He was again close to tears, and Mollie was going to hate both him and herself if he cried. She let out a long breath. She didn't approve of the war, hardly anyone did.

But she also didn't approve of getting out of it by illegitimate means. If a person felt strongly enough that participating in Vietnam was immoral, he had the option of going to jail or leaving the country. Mollie hoped that that was what she would do, if she had been subject to the draft; that, or fight. But not cheat out. But how could she know that she wouldn't have done exactly what Grady did if she had been in his shoes? How could she know how nobly she'd act if she were subject to the same pressures as he? She tried to think, but Grady rushed on:

"Miss Davis, I don't want to go. I know two guys killed already. I won't be in no officer's school, I'll go to Da Nang—"

"Please, hush a minute, Grady," Mollie said, not unkindly. "I know what you mean. Let me think."

She frowned at him. "You won't flunk out because of this one course, do you know? You have to flunk three courses to be kicked out. This is only one of them."

"I know," Grady said. "But this one . . . English I thought I could pass."

"By cheating." She let a silence stand. Grady studied the floor. One cheat judged another.

"I'll tell you what," she said. "I'll give you another chance. Come to my office Monday and you can write another essay. We'll forget this incident happened. But all right. If you pass on the second try, then as far as I'm concerned, you've passed the course."

"Thank you, thank you—" He did it, he did begin to cry.

"Don't thank me! You still have to write an essay that passes. I'm not giving you anything! If you don't write a passing essay, you flunk, and that's that. I suggest"—and here, horribly, Mollie gave him one of her beautiful smiles—"I suggest you study."

Grady did study. It was the longest weekend of his life. The term *Dead Week* took on new meaning. The English language—subjects, verbs, pronoun reference, all the horrors of Anglo-Saxon spelling—became charged with importance. He asked Mollie for help, and she tutored him for two hours on Saturday and three hours on Sunday. "Read it out loud, Grady," she urged, "and listen to yourself. Just write as you speak, and don't write anything you wouldn't say. You speak well enough." This wasn't precisely the truth, but she wanted him to have confidence. "Your dad's a principal. Surely he didn't raise an illiterate."

But he had.

On Monday, at ten in the morning, Grady Edwards turned in his essay. Attached to it was this postscript:

> Dear Mrs. Davs, I thanks you for this chanct
> giving myself this chanct. Again. This essay my own
> no one helping me. Plese tellafone me the grade I
> am very ~~ens~~ ansious to here. from you.
>> Yours sinseerly, Grady T. Edwards, Jr.

Reading his work, Mollie felt herself developing a migraine, not so much at Grady's prospects as at the total sense of failure she herself experienced. Thirty years later, remembering him, she felt ill again. Grady's essay—evaluated according to the standards set by the Freshman English Requirements Committee, but allowing for a few idiosyncrasies overlooked at the discretion of the instructor—Grady's essay scored, for grammar, development, and spelling, out of one hundred possible points, an absolute zero. The variety, quantity, and startling originality of the errors perpetrated by the young man were beyond the teacher's ability to forgive. She did not telephone Grady. She never spoke to him again, nor did she ever see him. She did what she felt was right, what she had to do to justify her actions both to herself and to the Freshman English Committee, in the unlikely event that the Committee ever inquired about her results, which she knew it wouldn't do. Grady Edwards went back to Denham Springs at the end of the fall semester, 1967. Whether he went to Da Nang, Mollie didn't know. She never heard of him again.

Mrs. Rowlander pressed the back of her hand to her forehead. The sun was just past noon, and the massive black granite of the wall had been absorbing heat all morning. Mollie knew that her husband wanted to go; she herself wanted to leave, but she felt she had to examine every one of the more than 57,000 names on the wall to assure herself that Grady's name wasn't there—or to verify that, in fact, it was. "I have to know," she said, fixing Mr. Rowlander with her glittering eye.

"You're being unreasonable," her husband said. "This is an exercise in masochism. What are you going to do if you find him? You told Grady Edwards the truth when you said that he had to fail three courses to flunk out. Yours was only one. He was asking you to cheat for him. And some other boy, someone just as vulnerable as Grady and maybe more so, who wasn't willing to cheat, that boy would have had to go in his place. You did the right thing."

"I know that," she said. "At least, I knew it then."

The wall stretched for nearly five hundred feet, with more than one hundred names to the foot. "I have to find him or not find him." She repeated simply, "I have to *know*." To make sure she didn't lose her place, she was touching the granite, keeping her location, feeling the letters engraved in the warm stone.

"Look at your hands," her husband said.

They were pressed so hard against the wall that the ends of her fingers were white.

"I'll go find a directory," Mr. Rowlander announced with authority. "That'll settle this in a few minutes."

Mollie looked down the wall, at the tens of thousands of names, at the wall's converging angles descending into the earth. The sun coruscated off the surface of the black granite; the names blurred in front of her. The letters could spell any name, they all turned into one. She could see her own face reflected in the highly polished stone, and she knew that she would never know what she needed to know: Never, whether or not she found Grady's name.

SPECULATION

$\mathcal{T}$he summer that Margaret and Harold worked on his house, the English ivy covering the oak tree in his back yard bloomed. The flowers smelled of green earth, a little funky; but, given the way that the ivy looped and swung from the tree's low-hanging limbs, Margaret thought it all quite beautiful. She liked the way the vines gave the tree an extra dimension. But she also noticed that the oak's topmost branches had lost most of their leaves.

"Your tree isn't getting enough oxygen," she told Harold. "It's being smothered."

"I don't know," Harold said. "The bees love the flowers."

Just the day before, they had discussed the fact that bees were endangered, so she didn't argue that point.

"But," she persisted, "the tree's dying."

"It won't look good if we strip it now." Harold was an architect, not a gardener like Margaret. He needed the property to look good, because once he'd finished renovating the house, he wanted it to sell fast. "Whoever buys it can deal with it," he said.

They both had enough to do that summer, so Margaret let it go. Besides, it was Harold's tree, Harold's house. He'd borrowed the money from his father to fix it up, and his father wanted interest—not much, but some—if Harold took more than six months to repay. The ivy stayed on the tree.

That was the summer Margaret wrote her first article, the water article. Besides teaching English full time and helping Harold fix up his house, she spent weekends researching the local water, trying to get the chemicals in it removed instead of discussed. The article was for a magazine called *Home & Health*, whose editor wanted something "easy to read, accessible."

"I want it to be as solid as anything in *Scientific American*," Margaret confided to Harold.

The city water works director showed her an atomic absorption unit. "This detects metals in water down to a ratio of .002 of a part per million," he explained. He assured Margaret, "The city has no problems with contamination."

But she also talked with a young chemist who had quit his job at the plant rather than continue putting 2,4-D into the city's surface water. Margaret interviewed public health professors, city engineers, and the *Chronicle*'s expert on the environment. Her congressman was spending the summer in Washington, but his deputy chief of staff took her to lunch. Over grilled hamburgers they talked into the afternoon about farming interests, runoff, chemical lobbies, money, and water. The senator's office put her in touch, toll-free, with EPA officials in Washington. Margaret ultimately drafted 160 pages of notes and spent scores of hours editing them.

"All this for a few hundred bucks and a byline?" Harold asked.

"If it's good enough," Margaret said, "it could make a difference. We're talking about an entire city's health."

By the time she read her final draft aloud to him, it was August. They worked on the house in the evenings, when it was cooler and the classes she taught were over for the day. She read while Harold sanded thirty years of grimy varnish off his kitchen cabinets, prepping them for painting.

"What do you think?" She laid her story on the kitchen counter. "I want your honest opinion."

He laughed and put down the sander. "That's what people say. They never mean it."

She knew he was joking, but it still felt like a puncture wound. "You don't like it?"

"Actually . . ." he said, drawling the syllables out, "it sounds like it ought to sound."

"Would you care to be more specific?"

"Margaret. It's ready. Stop. Stop worrying about the city and help me with this sanding, will you?"

Physical labor felt good, like everything else that year of physicality. They were twenty-two and twenty-seven years old. She'd go to Burger King on her way back from classes and bring Whoppers with a large order of fries to his house, with never a thought for cholesterol. They'd sit in the middle of the kitchen floor—that was the first room they finished, and at one point, thanks to Margaret, the floor *was* clean enough to eat from—and they'd eat; or, if it was decent weather, they'd spread a plaid cotton blanket outside under the oak. Nothing extraordinary happened during those months, except that Margaret felt happier and busier than she'd ever been.

Once she and Harold made love on an old mattress that had been left in the house, covering it first with a clean painter's dropcloth imported from the living room. It was late afternoon, with the blinds closed so that the room was almost, but not quite, dark. They could hear traffic crawling on the freeway five blocks distant—at seven o'clock it was still rush hour—and closer, cicadas shrilling loud and then louder in the trees. Afterwards, Margaret turned and pressed her face into the hollow between Harold's neck and his shoulder. "I can feel your eyelashes," he said. "You feel like a spider. A friendly one."

"When the weather gets hot," Margaret said, "we insects act up." She began to hum, pressing her lips against the side of his neck and imitating a kazoo.

"You can tell the temperature by the rate of insect activity," she added between hums. "Count the number of chirps . . . that a cricket makes during fifteen seconds . . . then add thirty-seven . . . and you get the temperature."

"Are you making this up?"

"Would I lie to you?"

"How would I know, if you're a good liar?"

They laughed together, like delighted children, or like two people in the first stage of romantic love. The room was warm and they started chirping and humming together, first old thirties and forties tunes, then any song they could think of containing the word "summer." When they ran out of "summer" they started on "moon": "Shine on Harvest —," "—light in Vermont," "— Over Miami," "No — at All," "— River," "By the Light of the Silvery —," "—glow," "Blue —," "—light Drive," "Fly Me to the —," "Old Devil —." The cicadas wound up outside and the room finally got dark. Then they made love again. After that Harold said he'd never finish the house at this rate and he thought he'd better paint a living room wall. That was the only time they ever made love in the house. Most of the time, she stayed at his apartment, or he at hers; or each went home alone.

A lawyer friend of Harold's who was settling a banker's estate had put him onto the house. It had stood empty for years, after being used for pot parties by the man's children in the early sixties, then rented for peanuts to a succession of tenants who'd left it stinking of dogs, with gouges in the wall patched over with newspaper. The floor in the add-on bedroom had rotted so much that Margaret could feel the wind shake up under the boards, and at first, mice inhabited the attic (or Norway rats; they sounded as big as puppies, although Margaret never saw them). Trash everywhere. Harold's lawyer friend had hinted during a racquetball game that the heirs weren't interested in fixing the place up, and that they would sell it dirt cheap. With prices the way they were in the Heights, somebody ought to cash in on it, he said. It was a bird's nest on the ground.

Harold hadn't been working on anything else; he had no job and no plan. Nearly a year earlier, he had quit a job in a forty-person firm because his boss had asked him to redo the stairs for a midtown office building. Harold had created a soaring design with a steel, glass, and clear polycarbonate escalator that showed the workings of the interior mechanism; but to create it would have put the building miles over budget. The partners admired it but needed something smaller, tighter. "They wanted a box," Harold said.

Before that, he'd been with a first-rate boutique firm in San Antonio, but when they'd had to cut back, he'd left Texas and moved to Oregon for a year, teaching architectural drawing at a respectable college east of the mountains, which was where he didn't want to be. "I don't want to grade other people's work," he said. "I want to create my own." But when he came back to Texas, all he did was work on his car for hours at a time. He lived on air, for all Margaret knew.

"So what do you *want*?" Margaret asked.

"I want to build cathedrals."

"Cathedrals have stairwells. You have to start somewhere."

"I didn't become an architect so I could indenture myself to philistines," he said.

She'd met Harold at a party to which everyone invited had been asked to bring the most interesting person they knew. Margaret's roommate, a fellow teacher, brought her. At some point, Margaret found herself perched on a barstool next to Harold, and over the course of a long evening they found that they were both from the same hometown and had gone to the same high school. Because Harold was a few years older, they'd never met. They both thought Aretha Franklin was the best singer/ songwriter ever and that television was a waste of time; Margaret learned that Harold was reading Jane Jacobs, and he discovered that Margaret was reading Betty Friedan. Each easily found the other the most interesting person in a room full of interesting people. When some weeks later Harold told Margaret he was renovating an old house and hinted that he could use a little help, she was happy to lend a hand.

But the house had to be sold even though after a while Margaret could imagine herself living in it, in those high airy rooms with the kind of dentate, real wood moldings you can't buy any more, and old wavy glass in some of the windows. She liked the oak in the back yard with its swags of ivy, and the sound of cicadas thrumming up hot and loud in the evenings. She didn't want the house to sell, and neither did Harold.

But he needed to pay his bills. He knocked out a wall between a closet-sized bedroom and the den, which opened a long space across the back of the house. He installed ceiling fans and French doors, four across, so that the shady back yard became an extension of the big den. In the rest of the house, he discovered good hardwood floors under orange shag so filthy it looked brown. But the best thing about the house was its light.

Shade-filtered sun slanted under wide eaves and through windows that had been designed to provide cross ventilation in a time before Houston became a city of air conditioning and fixed glass. "This window pane is violet," Margaret said, pulling up the old wooden venetian blinds that covered it. She loved the light and couldn't get enough of windows that reached almost floor to ceiling.

Harold outsourced the door frames and window moldings to Margaret, who scrubbed and scraped before he sanded. She washed fifty years of accumulated grime from a stove that hadn't been cleaned, she suspected, since the hippie children had used the oven like an indoor grill, coating it with hard layers of rippled grease. She took pleasure in seeing things come clean under her hands, but at one point she said to Harold, "You know what Nietzche says about cleanliness?"

"Mmmm." Harold had a nail between his lips, and he mumbled.

"Yes, *mmm*," she said. Like Harold, she liked working with her hands, and she didn't want to do just a cosmetic job. The house, neglected so long, deserved better. But she had begun to feel that he could do more than improve a place where other people would live. Margaret took off her rubber gloves. "Harold, you're putting more energy into painting cabinets than into your job-hunting."

On the other hand (and for Margaret, there was always an other hand, a compelling reason to think exactly the opposite of what she had thought one minute before), this house *was* Harold's job. The cabinet interiors, which he had lacquered a deep slate blue, contrasted dramatically with their white exteriors, and his good taste definitely added value. Margaret imagined the plates, cups, and saucers that the new owners would put inside those cabinets: white ironstone, her choice; or Fiestaware, his. Somebody was going to love this kitchen.

Her water article, which was supposed to come out in September, was postponed to October, by which time she and Harold had begun work on the outside of the house.

She taped the windows so he could paint a clean edge, and they marveled at the way window frames take four times longer to finish than anybody who has never painted one would guess. He chose a medium grey for the exterior, which made the most of the charcoal-colored roof and white trim. "The house looks like it's put on white tie," Margaret said, admiring their handiwork.

By that time the oak leaves were burned to a cheerless green, thickened like leather against the ninety-degree heat of a late Texas autumn. Harold talked about installing central air conditioning, but his money was almost gone and he decided that the ceiling fans were enough. If the people who bought the house couldn't live without refrigerated air, they could put it in themselves. The scraggly backyard roses, which Margaret had been cutting all summer, filling vases in Harold's apartment and her own, thrived for the abuse. She could imagine Harold at his drawing board in the light-saturated den at the back of the house, and herself preparing lessons or writing another article at a desk in the second bedroom. She wondered if he ever imagined this too. It seemed possible. But she never spoke of such things.

Harold talked about projects. As October progressed, he took time exposures of stars, he took pictures of clouds. He spoke at length of making a book about them, a book containing hundreds of photographs taken at fifteen-second intervals for hours, documenting a spectacular sunset, a huge Texas sky that would morph, page following page, into a shifting kaleidoscope of colors. What was more, he had an old college suitemate who was moving up fast in the publishing world, who had expressed an interest in issuing such a work. "What a fabulous opportunity," she said, "and you're the person to do it. Harold, do it!"

"Maybe I will," he said, but she was beginning to think he wouldn't. She didn't understand why, but he wouldn't. He was like one of those New Yorker cartoon characters who experiences life—a little pain, a little joy—but never acts on it.

Sometimes she looked at him sleeping. He had a bony face that was all cliffs and planes, a peaceful but cryptic landscape. Looking at him sleeping, it was easier for her to know why, when they were awake together, she could never say anything that really mattered. "Tell me you love me, Harold," she whispered to him in his sleep. "Or love *something.*"

In late October she began checking the newsstands for her water article. Every few days, after she and Harold had finished working on the house, they'd stop at a convenience store that carried magazines; once or twice they went to the big late-night newsstand on Bissonnet. But the issue was late, and by the first of November it still hadn't appeared.

"You'd think you were exposing Deep Throat," Harold told her. "You're so anxious."

"Deep Kidney," she said. "This is about water." She scouted drugstores, supermarkets, newspaper stands, any place she thought *Home & Health* might appear.

"Relax," Harold said. "It'll show up." But he knew how eager she was to see her first words in print, in multiple copies on the racks. He had to know, because she dragged him from newsstand to grocery to drugstore, night after night for two weeks.

After the fifth of November, she decided something horrible had happened. The magazine's editor had died, or its publisher had gone bankrupt, or the journal had folded.

"We're just running late," the magazine's secretary explained. "We'll certainly send you a copy."

Margaret was also suffering house blues. She and Harold had finished the renovation, painted the last topcoat, washed all the windows, cleaned up every speck and spatter. Nothing remained except to put up the For Sale by Owner sign, and Harold was readying that. Margaret made a pot of Lapsang souchong, not her favorite tea, but the only one in the house, and brought it to the patio where Harold was hand lettering a sign. She gave him a cup. "It's pretty smoky, but it's all we've got."

Harold was bent almost double over the sign, using an artist's sable-tipped brush too fine for the job. He was working on the *a* in *sale*. Over his head, the ivy quaked every time a breeze strayed, and a few more oak leaves drifted down.

"Would you like me to put your phone number on the sign?" he asked. "That way, if somebody calls, you can vet them and let me know."

"I'd just tell them to go away," she said.

"It'll look cleaner with just one number, I guess."

"There you go," she said politely.

"I can't drink this tea," he said. "Is there anything else?"

"Water. But don't drink that."

"God, no."

She wondered out loud how long Houston was going to accept a toxic herbicide in its water. The city dumped in 2,4-D, the young chemist who had quit his job explained, because of the water lilies. The lilies gave the water a bad taste, and people complained about that. "The 2,4-D made the lilies die, all right," the young chemist had said, "so people didn't complain anymore. But I just couldn't do it. I had to quit."

The advancing fall semester brought with it a storm of grading, record keeping, student conferences. Margaret taught a Monday night lecture followed by a two-hour lab that lasted until nine thirty. One night in mid-November, by the time she got to Harold's apartment, it was after ten.

"I hate night classes," she told him. "I'd rather be here."

"Here" was in bed with him, eating freshly popped corn and catching an old movie on television. Doris Day was lodging a complaint in *Pillow Talk* about Rock Hudson's monopoly of her party line, and Harold was scratching

Margaret's back, rubbing a little popcorn butter between her shoulder blades. "What's happened so far?" she asked.

"Absolutely nothing." He added, "I saw *Home & Health* today. At the hardware store."

"The hardware store?"

"I was picking up some turpentine. There were a bunch of copies in a rack at the checkout."

"Was my article in it?"

"Sure. There was even a picture, a black-and-white of a running faucet. A little overexposed."

"You didn't buy a copy?"

"They said they'd send you one."

"Harold, you know they haven't!"

"They will," he said, crunching on a half-popped kernel.

"You didn't want a copy for yourself?"

"I've already read it."

Finally, he saw her: Margaret swallowed hard, looked down, and wiped the corner of her eye. He looked away.

"I guess I should have bought one," he said. "They cost two-fifty."

"Two-fifty," she said, getting up.

Rock Hudson was pretending to be a rancher, so he could seduce Doris Day.

Margaret went into the bathroom and washed her face. When she reemerged, the movie was almost over. Harold said, "You want me to go out and get a copy?"

"At eleven o'clock? At the hardware store?"

Pillow Talk's credits rolled and they turned off the light. Harold went to sleep, but Margaret had a hard time drifting off. She had a waking dream of oaks and ivy; she was pulling down ivy, yards and yards of it. Sometimes she was tangled up in it, and sometimes she was the ivy itself. Sometimes it was Harold.

In the morning she left before he woke, taking with her the few things she kept at his apartment. She bought a copy of *Home and Health* at the Avalon Drugstore, then staked out a seat at the end of the counter and treated herself to French toast with two over-easy eggs and a fruit cup. She read her article through. There were no cuts, no typos, no changes. The magazine was handsome and glossy.

"What have you got there?" one of the counter staff asked, seeing Margaret smile. "You look mighty pleased."

"I *am* pleased," Margaret said. She held up the magazine in both hands and showed the waitress the spread. "I wrote this," she explained.

"Oh, my," the counterwoman said, studying the picture of the running faucet, the columns of even print.

Now Margaret felt a little silly and more than a little embarrassed. "It's just that I never published anything before," she said. "It's no big deal."

"Honey, don't say that," the waitress said. "Don't put yourself down." She nodded her head while she refilled

Margaret's coffee cup. "It ain't like a fried chicken flew in your mouth. Soak up the shine. Give yourself love."

Margaret leaned over the coffee cup and hugged her.

At the end of the week Harold told her that he had sold the house less than three days after he'd put the sign up. In fact, he sold it to a couple about their age who had been the first ones to look at it. "He's an engineer," he said, "and she teaches art. They can just swing the mortgage. But they're crazy about the place."

"They knew what they wanted and went for it," she said. "Let's wish them luck."

Later, she sometimes imagined that they were not unlike Harold and herself, except that they stayed in love.

DISTANCES, TIMING,
MEN & WOMEN

$\mathcal{T}$he day Margaret arrived in her hometown for Christmas, her mother gave her a letter. "It's been here a week," she said, "but I knew you were coming so I didn't forward it."

It was postmarked Seattle and addressed in a steeply vertical architectural lettering that Margaret recognized instantly. Her old friend Harold had written. Margaret was more curious than pleased, because the last time she'd talked with Harold—and that had been at least six years earlier—he had really put her off. She had been in Seattle on business, her first visit to that city, as well as her first travel in a new job. The company had put her up at the Four Seasons, where neither she nor Harold could have afforded even a drink back when they were a couple. By the time Margaret's work week ended, it was nearly nine o'clock. With nothing better to do, she checked the phone book to see if Harold still lived in Seattle. It didn't seem late, and she hoped he'd be glad to say hello or maybe even come to the Four Seasons for a drink. In truth, she was proud of her new job—she was directing research on the effects of acidic water on marine plants—and she wanted to show off a little.

A woman answered the phone, which was a surprise. "Is this Harold Morgan's residence?" Margaret asked.

It was.

"May I speak with him, please?"

"Who's calling?"

"This is Margaret Davis." She added, "I'm an old friend of Harold's."

There was an unnaturally long pause before the woman said, "Just a minute." She didn't sound friendly; she didn't even sound civil.

Harold came to the phone. "Harry!" Margaret cried, full of fading cheer. "This is Margaret. *Mollie.* I'm in Seattle and thought I'd give you a call and see how you're doing. So how are you doing?"

An energetic background racket began: somewhere an infant was yelping, pouring out pure infant id.

"I'm married now, Mollie." Harold's voice jumped over the noise. "My wife and I have a baby."

"Married! With a baby! That's great," Margaret said. "I can hear him."

"Her," he corrected. "The phone woke her up."

"I'm sorry." Margaret immediately felt contrite about the hour. "You used to go to bed so late."

"I'm not in bed, but the baby was. And my wife, too."

It was the same old Harold. Margaret couldn't deny that they had once had some wonderful times together, but whenever pressure got to him or he was inconvenienced the smallest amount, his mouth would contract to a lipless slit and he would articulate his words as if he were Martin Luther and she was the door where he nailed the ninety-five theses.

Margaret could have used a little indulgence. "I had no idea you were married," she said, "and we'll talk another time. Glad to hear you've set up a family again." This last was a dig, as Margaret meant it to be: Harold had been freshly divorced when she'd dated him and he already had one daughter by his first wife.

"Where are you?"

"The Four Seasons."

"I'll give you a call tomorrow."

"Don't bother," she said. "I'm leaving early."

"Well,"—and his consonants softened a bit—"I'll give you a call early."

After he hung up she rang the desk and said that she didn't want to be disturbed in the morning and could they please hold any calls? What did he think she had to say that he couldn't be polite for fifty seconds? Then for a few minutes she looked over the data collected that week, but decided that she would be fresher for work in the morning, on the plane. What is it with me, she wondered, for having spent nearly six months of my life with that man? She was tired but it took her a long time to go to sleep.

Now here in her mother's house at Christmas was Harold's letter. It was short, one page:

Mollie,

I don't know where you are but I hope this reaches you. My wife and I have finally and completely split up. We have an in-house separation. It should have been done six or seven years ago, or before we even got started.

I've thought about you a lot over the years. Our timing wasn't right, but I've never been able to forget you. I'd like to see you again or hear from you.

Hey, if you're married with five kids or otherwise not interested, please accept my best wishes.

Harold

What, she thought, is an in-house separation? Leave it to Harold to be too laid-back to even leave the house. As far as she was concerned, if he was still living in the same house as his wife, he was still married. There was a phone number she could call and an address, and that was the letter. She folded the paper and patted it back into the envelope.

Two seconds later she took it out and read it again. Several times, in fact.

Once upon a time, she was in love with him. And not just in love, *besotted*: under the influence, wildly infatuated, hammered with hormones, sloshed on sex (a new, welcome, and daring experience for her, if not for him).

Ah, Love! She was twenty-two years old and teaching English to the sons and daughters of middle-class Texans when a friend introduced her to Harold. He was tall, thin-lipped, agile, creative. An aesthete. It surprised her that he still had short hair.

"Let your hair grow," she advised. "Nobody wears it that way anymore."

"You don't like it?" he said, his eyebrows astonished.

"You'll look handsomer if you let it grow." She ran her hand over the top of his head. "Let it grow," she said.

He let it grow.

She loved his conversation, his long skinny Texas body; and she held him in thrall with her own (plus her best friend's philosophy of mesmerization by eye contact: focus on a man's right eye, then on his left; alternate the focus at long intervals and *listen*; few men will fail to believe that they are in fascinating company). He was her first love; she could imagine no other. And unlike the children of the era's zeitgeist, when even the recently widowed first lady was photographed with her nipples perked, and Margaret's contemporaries were dancing at Woodstock covered mostly by body paint, Margaret dreamed of begonias at the doorstep, beef stews steaming the kitchen.

But Harold was freshly divorced and smarting; and Margaret was of the opinion that once in a while, he could listen to *her*. Not only did he not share her dreams, he had no interest in learning what they were. So when her teacher's contract expired, she fled to graduate school instead of staying in Houston, and Harold moved to Seattle. The only address she left was her mother's. It was a clean break. They were friends but she didn't see him again. For a year or two, they talked on the phone now and then, and he invited her for a visit that she declined; then there was the night that she had called him from the Four Seasons. Now, six years after that, here was his letter. Twelve years ago she had thought she loved him. Six years ago, she still felt good about him. Now what she remembered most from their entire association was that brush-off on the phone.

Harold's letter wasn't the only memorabilia Margaret encountered on her Christmas trip home. She and her mother were invited to a big Christmas brunch crowded with people Margaret didn't know or hadn't seen in decades. They were her mother's friends, not hers, but her mother wanted her to go.

"I just hope," Margaret said, "that nobody interrogates me about why I'm not married."

"Who would do that?"

"Everybody does that."

"Well," her mother advised cheerfully, "tell them you'll reveal your secret if they'll tell you why their first marriage failed."

Margaret needn't have worried. The hostess had lively friends, an industrious bartender, and a buffet loaded with all Margaret's favorites: crab fingers, boiled shrimp in remoulade hot with horseradish, ham, roast beef, lemon chess pie! and even a few items that might be called healthy, which everyone ignored. Debating whether a third rum ball would roll off her plate or whether she should just come back later for more, Margaret found herself standing next to a small but trim man in his forties. He was shorter than she was, but elegant in a gray suit and Ferragamos with an old-pewter shine. Gray hair, glasses, fine expressive and gentle features. The woman with him had a beautiful smile and perfect white even teeth.

"You remember Cecil, don't you, Mollie?" Margaret's mother materialized from nowhere and grasped the man's hand, holding it aloft in both of her own. "Cecil Stander, who used to visit his grandparents next door?"

"Cecil Stander!" Margaret exclaimed. An apparition. The love of her childhood, her own supernova. When Margaret was six, Cecil Stander had showed her how to ride a two-wheeler. When she was seven, standing on his saddle oxfords, he taught her the box step. When she was eight and he ran over her cat (which had been sleeping under his car), he cried with her. And when she was nine, he left to go fight the North Koreans. Eagle Scout, highest-ranking student in Coahoma County, Mississippi, he had signed up at seventeen for Army training. She had thought she'd never see him again. Now he stood before her in a gray vested suit, holding a Cutty Sark in his left hand as Margaret's mother continued to clasp his right.

"I wouldn't have recognized you," he said. "You were such a little kid." He turned to his wife, who was beaming in the manner of advanced-hour Christmas parties. "My grandparents lived next door to the Davises when Mollie was . . ." He paused. "Well, it's been over twenty years, hasn't it?"

"More than twenty-five," Margaret said.

"My goodness!" said Mrs. Stander, displaying her beautiful teeth.

Margaret regarded her with a twinge of envy. "Cecil, what has happened for you in the last twenty-five years?"

He smiled with the modest self-deprecation affordable in a man surrounded by three admiring women.

Had he said he was a Nobel laureate, the guardian of white whales, or Machiavelli's corporate prince, Margaret couldn't have listened more attentively, and without thinking once of left-eye, right-eye technique. "Ah, Cecil!" she said, the words inflected as *Aren't you wonderful.*

She could remember (and wasn't about to mention it) lying awake after her bedtime and looking past the azaleas that separated Cecil's home from her parents'. He lived on the second story of his grandparents' house on Letitia Street and his room was across the driveway, about twelve feet up. Often Cecil arrived home just before Margaret went to sleep in the long summer twilights; the cicadas would be thrumming their stout sub-tropical complaints. Cecil would flick on his bathroom light and Margaret could see everything above the high window sill: the wallpaper printed with green ivy leaves; the border, plain white; the ceiling, discolored with bronze water stains. The lamp over the mirror (which Margaret presumed hung over the sink, although the basin was out of sight) was one of those crook-necked imitation-Tiffany flowers, pale rose translucent petals over a single bulb. Cecil would peer into his bathroom mirror under this light and perform delicate bathroom surgeries upon his pimply chin. Finishing this, he'd brush his teeth. What a toothbrusher! Cecil brushed for minutes at a time, which, it now occurred to Margaret, was perhaps one reason he had married his wife, with the beautiful teeth. He put muscle into oral hygiene. Toothpaste foamed around his lips and chin. It ran down his fist, proceeded south in rivulets upon his forearm, dripped from his elbow. There he'd wipe from time to time with a towel. Then he'd go on brushing.

After that he'd disappear off to the right, presumably into the shower, which Margaret also couldn't see. When he came out he'd be toweling his shoulders, back, and chest, which were as white and hairless as linoleum. Then he'd attend to his coiffure, toweling his hair vigorously, then slicking back the sides with brush, comb, and Brylcreem (using, indeed, just a little dab). The hair on top, which was longer, needed coaxing until a wavy pompadour emerged with a side-leaning forelock; then a touch more pomade, until Cecil—or his hair, at least—looked like James Dean, leading heartthrob of the 1950s. The sight of Cecil torturing his quiff was the high point of Margaret's night's vigil, if she could stay awake long enough to watch. Unfortunately, Cecil often spent so much time in the shower that she fell asleep despite herself.

Mornings, about the time she knew he'd be doing his chores, she'd manage to be picking azaleas from the hedge that separated her parents' house from his. For this there was a reward: Cecil spoke. True, he seldom said more than "Hi, Birdlegs," but she knew from his affectionate intonation that if he'd just wait for her to grow up—fifteen years at the outside, ten if he was in a hurry—they would be best friends forever. But when Margaret was nine, Cecil left, giving her his "I Like Ike" button as a parting remembrance. She kept it for weeks next to her hamster cage and then it disappeared, stolen, she remembered thinking, by the communists.

The seventeen-year-old Cecil, combed, carbuncular, and clean, materialized in the hazy recall of childhood. Cecil, Margaret wanted to say, if you had known, all those years ago, how much I admired you, wouldn't you have come back? She would have been more careful, for her own part, about toothbrushing.

"Your mother says you're doing ocean research," Cecil was saying, Cutty Sark in hand. "How did a girl from Letitia Street get interested in that?"

"My dad gave me *Kon-Tiki* when I was ten," she said. "I wanted to know where Polynesia was."

He looked interested and smiled. He still had gorgeous teeth.

The evening after the big Christmas brunch, hours after Margaret and her mother had returned home to another enormous meal (there was no getting away from it), and assisted by a big glass of pinot noir, Margaret lay on the maple bed where she had slept as a child and composed three drafts of a reply to Harold. She was elevated ("There is a time to every purpose") and affected ("Readiness is all") and clichéd ("A matter of time"). Six ounces of vino could not disguise the sad inadequacy of these responses. Margaret decided to let bygones be bygones, but she could think of nothing she wanted to say. She gave it up and went back down to the kitchen, where she discovered her mother polishing off the remains of a turkey leg. The older woman spooned a helping of cornbread-and-sausage dressing onto two small plates, while Margaret poured most of the remaining pinot noir into two glasses.

"I'm dating a new man," she said.

"Someone interesting?"

"Yes. His name is Raymond Rowlander. He's the youngest full professor of physics who's ever taught at the university."

"Mmmm!" her mother said, chewing.

There was a silence, and then Margaret said, without preamble, "Mama, what's the matter with me? Everybody I know, I'm talking about the entire universe here, is married except me. Two by two, eventually everybody goes into the ark. I might as well be wearing a teeshirt that says, Give me your narcissists, your egoists, your mama's boys, your self-righteous bullshitters, your married predators, your unproductive artists, your players who are never on time. I've met them all! What's the matter with me?"

Her mother looked thoughtful as she took another bite.

"Most men want an open vagina and a closed mouth," Margaret said.

"That may be more information than I'm ready for."

"They want a pretty doormat who never, ever, has needs of her own."

"You're the one picking them," her mother observed, "and you don't become a doormat without lying down first." She leveled a blue gaze at Margaret. "Are you afraid of getting married?"

"I'm afraid of getting divorced."

Her mother considered, and was silent again.

"You and Dad were so happy," Margaret continued. "So normal. How did you know he was the one?"

"When it's right, you just know. You don't have to ask anyone."

"I've never experienced that."

"Tell me about this new man," her mother said. "What's wrong with *him*?"

"Actually," Margaret said, "he seems extremely nice." She told her mother about her first date with Professor Raymond Rowlander. He had made reservations for dinner at seven o'clock at Margaret's favorite restaurant in Rice Village. But around two that afternoon it had begun to rain, one of Houston's infamous storms. It wasn't just rain: the sky opened and sheets of water flooded the city's underpasses and filled its bayous to the tops of their banks. From her second-story window, Margaret watched as the street in front of her townhouse became impassable. And the rain continued to fall.

"The thing is," she told her mother, "it was clearly impossible for anyone to get to my place. That was understandable.

What was not understandable was that he didn't call to let me know."

"His phone wasn't working?"

"I was trying to tell myself that, and not having a lot of success, when, at exactly twelve minutes after seven, he rang my doorbell. He had a huge umbrella, but he was soaked, dripping all over the floor, but he was *there*, you know, in that weather, holding his shoes so they wouldn't be ruined and apologizing for being twelve minutes late. It turned out he had lived in the neighborhood for years, so he knew all the high safe streets, and when the rain finally quit, which took hours—thank God I had crackers and a bottle of wine on hand—we went out and while we were in the restaurant it started raining again and along with everybody there we were trapped until three in the morning. And I never had a better time in my life."

"He *does* sound interesting."

"Ray says he's been fortunate in life," Margaret said, "and he's grateful for his good fortune."

"Like your father."

The conversation then shifted to that perfect man, whom they both missed very much.

Finally Margaret's mother said, "I need to go to bed. Long day!"

When Margaret returned to her bedroom, taking an injudicious last glass of pinot noir with her, Harold's letter lay face up on the bed. She decided to telephone him. She knew she had never been in love with him, not real love, despite her violent infatuation; but she had never forgotten him, either. She picked up her mother's landline and dialed. Then she pressed the off button on the first ring. After ten ounces of wine, she could have said anything.

Five seconds later, her own phone rang. She considered not answering; answering was clearly unwise; she definitely would not answer. On the fifth ring, she answered.

"It will never happen," she said into the receiver.

A startled voice asked, "Margaret?"

"Oh!" Margaret said. "*Raymond!*" Over the long-distance wires his voice was as sweet as "Silent Night." "I thought you were somebody else!"

"That's obvious," he said genially. "Should I hang up?"

"No no no no. Merry Christmas. Absolutely do not hang up."

While Margaret continued to sip pinot noir, Raymond told her about all the work he'd been able to accomplish while his colleagues and students weren't there to interrupt him. She told him about running into her childhood's brilliant boy next door who had translated Korean for MacArthur.

"I was wondering," Ray eventually said, "if I could persuade you to fly back tomorrow morning. I don't want to wait until New Year's Eve to see you."

"I don't either! But I could never get a flight tomorrow. Everything's bound to be booked."

"There's a United out of Baton Rouge at nine fifteen," he said, "with seats available. I checked before I called you. I could reserve it for you."

The wine in her system made him seem much farther away than four hundred miles. She lay on her bed with her eyes closed and wished her head weren't full of fog. "My mother hasn't seen me for ages . . ."

"She saw you in August. I'll meet your plane."

Her left bedpost split into a twin of itself and drifted northeast and southwest. She made a firm decision to give up wine for Lent, knowing she would never give up anything for Lent, and watched with a certain interest to see if her bedpost would rejoin itself.

"Margaret?"

"Sorry. Thinking."

"Let's go for brunch," Ray said. "No rain tomorrow."

The twinned post of Margaret's bed returned to its proper place. "I told my mom I'd be staying."

"So go back at spring break," Ray persisted. "I'll come with you."

Margaret turned and looked out the window. The azalea hedge was still there, although Cecil's family had moved long ago. The second-story bathroom window where she had watched her teenaged hero brush his teeth was dark.

She wondered if the ivy-leaved wallpaper still hung down in the corner. Then she rolled back over, wrinkling the three drafts of her impossible responses to Harold. She would never answer Harold's letter; there was no longer anything to say. She hoped Harold would assume his letter had never reached her.

"But," Ray continued, "you could ask your mother."

"I don't need to ask anyone," Margaret said. She felt inexplicably happy. "Ten thirty? You'll be on time?"

Raymond Rowlander laughed. "I'm always on time."

Reader, he was.

ACKNOWLEDGMENTS

$\mathcal{T}$he first person I want to thank is my husband, Jim Colthart, for forty years of unconditional love. Jim, for your unwavering support of my work, for excellent advice (and almost always only when asked) and for the depth and breadth of your insight into all things literary, I am forever grateful.

To Chris and Lara Colthart, thank you for giving me the best possible reason to gather these stories into a book. I hope Wren will read them when she grows up, and find in them her Grandma Jackie's voice.

To Eileen O'Leary and Jane Falion, for bringing "Sisters" to the Riverwalk Theatre. You delivered unforgettable joy.

To Karen Jewell, for casting a killer eye on my errors. Any that remain sneaked in after you looked.

To the readers of this book: *Thank you.*

ABOUT THE AUTHOR

Jacqueline Simon has won four awards for short stories which appear in this book: "If He Could Speak to His Brother" was a 1984 finalist for the National Magazine Award for Fiction, "Sisters" received a grant from the Texas Commission on the Arts, "Cheats" gained the Cultural Arts Council of Houston's Creative Artist Award, and "Leaving Letitia Street" won PEN Southwest's first Houston Discovery Prize. Her stories have appeared in *Ploughshares, Redbook, Domestic Crude* (renamed *Gulf Coast*), other journals, and the anthology *Her Work*. She has taught creative writing at almost every level, from Houston's Bellaire High School to Rice University's Glasscock School. She and her husband, James Colthart, live in Houston and New Hampshire.